PAUL TEMPLE
AND THE
JONATHAN MYSTERY

Francis Durbridge

WILLIAMS & WHITING

Cover design by Timo Schroeder

9781912582990

Williams & Whiting (Publishers)
15 Chestnut Grove, Hurstpierpoint,
West Sussex, BN6 9SS

Titles by Francis Durbridge published by Williams & Whiting

1   The Scarf – tv serial
2   Paul Temple and the Curzon Case – radio serial
3   La Boutique – radio serial
4   The Broken Horseshoe – tv serial
5   Three Plays for Radio Volume 1
6   Send for Paul Temple – radio serial
7   A Time of Day – tv serial
8   Death Comes to The Hibiscus – stage play
    The Essential Heart – radio play
    (writing as Nicholas Vane)
9   Send for Paul Temple – stage play
10 The Teckman Biography – tv serial
11 Paul Temple and Steve – radio serial
12 Twenty Minutes From Rome – a teleplay
13 Portrait of Alison – tv serial
14 Paul Temple: Two Plays for Radio Volume 1
15 Three Plays for Radio Volume 2
16 The Other Man – tv serial
17 Paul Temple and the Spencer Affair – radio serial
18 Step In The Dark – film script
19 My Friend Charles – tv serial
20 A Case For Paul Temple – radio serial
21 Murder In The Media – more rediscovered serials and
    stories
22 The Desperate People – tv serial
23 Paul Temple: Two Plays for Television
24 And Anthony Sherwood Laughed – radio series
25 The World of Tim Frazer – tv serial
26 Paul Temple Intervenes – radio serial
27 Passport To Danger! – radio serial
28 Bat Out of Hell – tv serial
29 Send For Paul Temple Again – radio serial

Murder At The Weekend – the rediscovered newspaper serials and short stories

Also published by Williams & Whiting:
Francis Durbridge : The Complete Guide
By Melvyn Barnes

Titles by Francis Durbridge to be published by Williams & Whiting

Breakaway – The Local Affair
Johnny Washington Esquire
Murder On The Continent (Further re-discovered serials and stories)
One Man To Another – a novel
Operation Diplomat
Paul Temple and the Alex Affair
Paul Temple and the Canterbury Case (film script)
Paul Temple and the Conrad Case
Paul Temple and the Geneva Mystery
Paul Temple and the Lawrence Affair
Paul Temple and the Margo Mystery
Paul Temple: Two Plays For Radio Vol 2 (Send For Paul Temple and News of Paul Temple)
The Passenger
Tim Frazer and the Salinger Affair
Tim Frazer and the Mellin Forrest Mystery

INTRODUCTION

Those not familiar with the multi-faceted career of Francis Durbridge (1912-98) might welcome a brief account. He began in 1933 as a writer of sketches, stories and plays for BBC radio, mostly light entertainments, but a talent for crime fiction became evident in his early radio plays *Murder in the Midlands* (1934) and *Murder in the Embassy* (1937).

Although Durbridge continued to write plays and serials for BBC radio for many years, using his own name and the pseudonyms Frank Cromwell, Nicholas Vane and Lewis Middleton Harvey, he became best known for creating the dream team of novelist/detective Paul Temple and his wife Steve. The audience reaction to his radio serial *Send for Paul Temple* led to sequels over several decades that secured an impressive UK and European fanbase. So following *Send for Paul Temple* in 1938, Durbridge responded later the same year with *Paul Temple and the Front Page Men* and continued with many more. From 1939 to 1968 there were another twenty-six Paul Temple cases, of which seven were new productions of earlier broadcasts.

Then in 1952, while continuing to write for radio, Durbridge embarked on a run of BBC television serials that attracted huge viewing figures until 1980. And additionally, from 1971 in the UK and even earlier in Germany, he became known for intriguing stage plays that were not simply whodunits but more in the style of Frederick Knott's *Dial M for Murder* or Ira Levin's *Deathtrap*.

Paul Temple and the Jonathan Mystery was first broadcast on the BBC Light Programme in eight thirty-minute episodes from Thursday 10 May to Thursday 28 June 1951, and the episodes were repeated on Friday each week. With Temple played by Kim Peacock (1901-66), it was the fourteenth outing for Temple and Steve. Although Peacock had a long run in the role, beginning in 1946 with *Paul Temple and the Gregory Affair* and ending in 1953 with the one-hour play *Paul Temple and Steve Again*, he was replaced by Peter Coke (1913-2008) for *Paul Temple and the Gilbert Case* (1954). Coke then made Temple his own in the ten subsequent serials until the concluding *Paul Temple and the Alex Affair* in 1968.

Marjorie Westbury (1905-89), as Steve Temple, partnered both Peacock and Coke in all their appearances, and before Peacock she had played Steve opposite Barry Morse in *Send for Paul Temple Again* (1945) and Howard Marion-Crawford in *A Case for Paul Temple* (1946). In total she was Steve on twenty-two occasions until the final serial *Paul Temple and the Alex Affair* (1968) – which coincidentally was a new production of her first appearance as Steve in the 1945 *Send for Paul Temple Again*. But mention must also be made of Lester Mudditt, who appeared nineteen times as Sir Graham Forbes of Scotland Yard from the original serial in 1938 until *Paul Temple and the Spencer Affair* (1957-58).

A new production of *Paul Temple and the Jonathan Mystery* was broadcast in eight thirty-minute episodes on the BBC Light Programme from 14 October to 2 December 1963, with Peter Coke playing Temple for the ninth time. This was repeated on the BBC Home Service from Monday 14 December to Wednesday 23 December 1964, rather unusually at 10.30 on each weekday morning. It was broadcast yet again on the BBC Home Service from 6 January to 24 February 1967, and since 2004 it has been frequently repeated on BBC Radio 7 and its successor BBC Radio 4 Extra. This 1963 production has also been marketed on audiocassettes and CDs (BBC Audio, 2004) and included in the CD box set *Paul Temple: The Complete Radio Collection: The Sixties 1960-1968* (BBC, 2017).

Turning to Paul Temple's career on the Continent, the Dutch radio version was *Paul Vlaanderen en het Jonathan mysterie* (25 January to 29 March 1953, eight episodes), translated by J.C. van der Horst and produced by Kommer Kleijn, with Jan van Ees as Vlaanderen and Eva Janssen as Ina; the German radio version was *Paul Temple und der Fall Jonathan* (17 September to 5 November 1954, eight episodes), translated by Elfriede Engelmann and produced by Eduard Hermann, with René Deltgen as Temple and Annemarie Cordes as Steve; and the Italian radio version was *Chi è Jonathan?* (12 to 23 April 1971, ten episodes), translated by Franca Cancogni and produced by Umberto Benedetto, with Mario Feliciani as Temple and Lucia Catullo as Steve.

The Temples also proved popular with cinemagoers in the era of black-and-white British crime movies. They were played by Anthony Hulme and Joy Shelton in *Send for Paul Temple* (1946, based on the original 1938 radio serial); John Bentley and Dinah Sheridan in the two films *Calling Paul Temple* (1948, based on the 1945 radio serial *Send for Paul Temple Again*) and *Paul Temple's Triumph* (1950, based on the 1939 radio serial *News of Paul Temple*); and John Bentley and Patricia Dainton in *Paul Temple Returns* (1952, based on the 1942 radio serial *Paul Temple Intervenes*). These films have been preserved by Renown Pictures, are shown regularly on Talking Pictures TV, and were collected as the DVD box set *The Paul Temple Collection Limited Edition* (Renown Pictures, 2011).

As with many of Durbridge's radio and television serials, *Paul Temple and the Jonathan Mystery* was novelised – but many years after it was first broadcast, and it was not a straight adaptation. While *Dead to the World* (Hodder & Stoughton, March 1967) retains the plot of the radio serial, all the character names are changed and the Temples are replaced by photographer Philip Holt and his secretary Ruth Sanders. It has been published in Germany as *Der Siegelring*, in France as *Sous le signe du dollar*, in Italy as *Morto per il mondo*, in the Netherlands as *De zegelring* and in Poland as *Umarły dla świata*. And lovers of audiobooks can hear *Dead to the World* read by Neil Pearson on CDs (AudioGo, 2013).

Melvyn Barnes
Author of *Francis Durbridge: The Complete Guide* (Williams & Whiting, 2018)

This book reproduces Francis Durbridge's original script together with the list of characters and actors of the BBC programme on the dates mentioned, but the eventual broadcast might have edited Durbridge's script in respect of scenes, dialogue and character names.

PAUL TEMPLE
AND THE
JONATHAN MYSTERY

A serial in eight episodes
By FRANCIS DURBRIDGE
Broadcast on BBC Radio
10 May – 28 June 1951

CAST:

Paul Temple . . . . .Kim Peacock
Steve, his wife . . . . . Marjorie Westbury
Sir Graham Forbes . . . . .Lester Mudditt
Robert Ferguson . . . . George Margo
Helen Ferguson . . . . . . Grizelda Hervey
Reggie Mackintosh . . Duncan McIntyre
Dinah Nelson . . . . Belle Crystall
Mavis Russell . . . . Rita Vale
Inspector Gerrard . . . . .Stanley Groome
Charlie . . . . .Frank Partington
Red Harris . . . . .Frank Atkinson
Rudolf Charles . . . . .Olaf Olsen
Mark Elliot . . . . .Martin Lewis
Eddie Paget . . . . Charles Lefeaux
Hotel porter . . . . Leslie Parker
Richard Ferguson . . . . .David Peel
Mrs Parsons . . . . .Courtney Hope
Max Wyman . . . . .Michael Holt

Other parts played by Gabrielle Blunt,
Arthur Bush, Frank Coburn, Roger Delgado,
Hamilton Dyce, Spencer Hale, Malcolm Hayes,
Harry Hutchinson, Bryan Powley, Alan Reid,
Ronald Sidney, Dorothy Smith and Lewis Ward

NEW PRODUCTION
Broadcast on BBC Radio
14 October – 2 December 1963
CAST:

Paul Temple . . . . Peter Coke
Steve, his wife . . . . . Marjorie Westbury
Robert Ferguson . . . . .John Glen
Helen Ferguson . . . . . . Grizelda Hervey
Charlie . . . . James Beattie
Inspector Gerrard . . . . . . .Rolf Lefebvre
Sir Graham Forbes . . . James Thomason
Dinah Nelson . . . . . . Valerie Kirkbright
Reggie Mackintish . . . . Simon Lack
Simo . . . . Lee Fox
Red Harris . . . . .John Baddeley
Police Sergeant . . . . . . Frederick Treves
B.O.A.C. Steward . . . . Frederick Treves
Customs Officer . . . . . Frederick Treves
Mrs Parsons . . . . .Eva Stuart
Max Wyman . . . . .Frederick Treves
Hall Porter . . . . Frank Partington
Rudolf Charles . . . . Anthony Hall
Mavis Russell . . . . Isabel Rennie
Mark Elliot . . . . William Fox
Richard Ferguson . . . . . .Gabriel Woolf
Phone Operator . . . . .James Beattie
Waiter . . . . James Beattie
Bobby, a bartender . . . . .David Spenser
Eddie Paget . . . . John Baddeley
Mrs Gulliver . . . . . Vivienne Chatterton
Police Messenger . . . . Peter Bartlett
Car Driver . . . . .Peter Bartlett
Peggy . . . . Jo Manning Wilson
Police Officer . . . . Glyn Dearman

Fireman . . . . .Alan Haines

Sergeant . . . . Alan Haines

Edward . . . . James Beattie

Porter . . . . .James Beattie

Porter . . . . Glyn Dearman

Doctor . . . . Lewis Stringer

Waiter . . . . Lewis Stringer

Hall Porter . . . . .Lewis Stringer

Phone Operator . . . . . .Valerie Kirkbright

Clerk . . . . Peter Bartlett

Milson . . . . .Lewis Stringer

1st Immigration Officer . .Frank Partington

2nd Immigration Officer .Frederick Treves

EPISODE ONE

THE FERGUSONS

OPEN TO:

FADE UP the noise of a Boeing. It is a B.O.A.C. en-route from New York to London.

Slow FADE IN the buzz of background conversation.

TEMPLE: Tired, Steve?

STEVE: No, not a bit. I'm just excited.

TEMPLE: You've been excited ever since the plane left New York.

STEVE: It's the thought of going home. What time do we arrive in London?

TEMPLE: About nine o'clock. (*Laughing*) So relax!

STEVE: These planes are marvellous, aren't they? They've got everything except the kitchen stove!

TEMPLE: Darling, they've got the kitchen stove!

STEVE: Of course you would be difficult!

TEMPLE: I've got a thirst, let's go up to the little lounge and have a drink.

STEVE: By all means.

FADE DOWN background conversation.

FADE UP ROBERT FERGUSON. He is a fairly well-educated American businessman; almost fifty-three or four.

ROBERT: (*Pleasantly*) Pardon me! But I think you're sitting on my magazine …

STEVE: Oh, I'm so sorry!

ROBERT: No, please, don't get up!

STEVE: But I'm sure I've got your seat!

ROBERT: No! No, really!

HELEN: (*From the near background: an educated English voice: about the same age as Robert*) Sit down, Robert, and don't make such a fuss!

ROBERT: I'm not making a fuss, Helen! (*Chuckling*) We're flying the Atlantic – this isn't a bus on 42nd

3

Street. I guess there's plenty of seats for everybody …

HELEN: There won't be if you put your magazines on them.

TEMPLE and STEVE laugh.

ROBERT: Trust my wife to have the last word! By the way, my name is Ferguson – Robert Ferguson.

TEMPLE: Mine's Temple … this is my wife.

HELEN: Not Paul Temple?

TEMPLE: Yes, I'm afraid so.

HELEN: Darling, I knew I was right! I told you, didn't I? I recognised you at the airport, Mr Temple. I never forget a face, do I, Robert?

ROBERT: Never. (*To TEMPLE*) She thought you were Cary Grant.

STEVE: I wish he was Cary Grant!

They all laugh.

TEMPLE: Is this your first trip to England?

ROBERT: Oh no, I've been over many times. My wife lived in London until we were married.

TEMPLE: Are you coming over on business, Mr Ferguson?

ROBERT: Well – not entirely.

HELEN: We've got a boy at Oxford – he'll be twenty-one the day after tomorrow.

STEVE: Oh, how nice!

TEMPLE: What college?

ROBERT: He's at Magdalen.

TEMPLE: Oh, that's my old college.

ROBERT: Is that so? D'you hear that, Helen, Mr Temple was at Magdalen.

HELEN: (*Busy talking to Steve*) Yes, I heard, darling. (*To STEVE*) Here's a photograph of Richard, Mrs Temple. It was taken last year.

A moment.

4

STEVE:	He's certainly good looking, Mrs Ferguson – you must be very proud of him.
HELEN:	We are,
STEVE:	He doesn't look very American, does he?
ROBERT:	You can hardly call him an American, Mrs Temple. He's been at school in England since he was twelve.
HELEN:	Richard adores England.
ROBERT:	You're telling me! Every time we suggest he comes back to the States we come over to England. (*He laughs*)
STEVE:	What's he going to do when he comes down from Oxford?
HELEN:	I think he's going to be a writer. His letters are full of books he's read and things he's written.
ROBERT:	(*Dubiously*) Yeah …
HELEN:	Oh, I know what you want, Robert. You want him to go into that beastly business of yours, but I don't believe in forcing a boy into doing anything he doesn't want to do. It's a great mistake. Don't you agree, Mrs Temple?
STEVE:	Well …
ROBERT:	If Richard wants to be a writer – o.k. he's a writer! But if he does decide to go into the old firm – well – it would make me very happy.
HELEN:	Yes, well he won't go into the old firm – you know he won't. Now I ask you, Mrs Temple! Fancy sending a boy to Oxford and then putting him in the furniture business!
ROBERT:	Now listen, Helen, don't get any high falutin' ideas! I didn't go to Oxford and your old man didn't. And if it comes to that Abe Lincoln didn't go to Oxford either and he got by all right!

TEMPLE and STEVE laugh.

5

STEWARD: Excuse me, sir. Your drinks …

TEMPLE: Oh, thank you. (*Handing over a drink*) Steve …

STEVE: Thank you, dear.

TEMPLE: Will you and Mrs Ferguson join us?

ROBERT: That's very kind of you, but we've got ours here.

TEMPLE: Well, here's to a pleasant trip, Mr Ferguson.

ROBERT: Thank you.

STEVE: And to your son – Richard. Happy birthday!

HELEN: Oh, how kind of you!

ROBERT: Mighty kind. Thank you, Mrs Temple.

TEMPLE: (*Clinking his glass on STEVE's*) To Richard …

FADE UP of music.

FADE DOWN of music.

FADE UP background noises and conversation of the Arrivals Lounge at London Airport.

CUSTOMS
OFFICER: Have you anything else to declare, sir?

TEMPLE: No. No, nothing else.

CUS. OFF: What about the briefcase – is that yours?

TEMPLE: Yes. It's full of papers – business documents. There's nothing else in it. I'll open it if you like.

CUS. OFF: No, that's all right, Mr Temple. Thank you.

TEMPLE: Thank you. All right, Steve.

A pause.

STEVE: Did he open your brief case?

TEMPLE: No.

STEVE: (*Casually*) Good.

TEMPLE: Why?

STEVE: I put my nylons in there.

TEMPLE: What! Well, Steve, really … You women!

STEVE: (*Quickly*) Oh, there's Charlie!

TEMPLE: Where?

STEVE: Hello, Charlie!

6

CHARLIE: Good morning, Mrs T. Good morning, sir! Welcome home!

TEMPLE: Thank you, Charlie! Have you got the car?

CHARLIE: Yes, sir. It's all ready, sir. Everything's oke – (*Correcting himself*) – on the beam, sir. I'll take the zip, Mrs T. You 'ang onto the hatbox.

GERRARD: (*An educated voice. Middle fifties*) Good morning, Mr Temple.

TEMPLE: (*Surprised*) Oh, hello, Inspector!

GERRARD: Have you just arrived from New York?

TEMPLE: Yes. Do you know my wife, Inspector? Darling, this is Inspector Gerrard. One of Sir Graham's bright boys.

STEVE: How d'ya do.

GERRARD: How do you do, Mrs Temple. You say you've just flown in from New York?

TEMPLE: Yes.

GERRARD: On flight 508?

TEMPLE: Yes, that's right.

GERRARD: Well, you must have travelled over with a Mr and Mrs Ferguson.

STEVE: Yes. As a matter of fact we did.

GERRARD: What does he look like?

TEMPLE: That's Ferguson over there, the tall man with the brown overcoat.

STEVE: Are you looking for them?

GERRARD: Yes.

TEMPLE: Why?

GERRARD: I'm afraid I've got some very bad news for them. Their son was murdered – last night …

Dramatic FADE UP of music.

FADE DOWN of music.

7

FADE UP the voices of SIR GRAHAM FORBES and INSPECTOR GERRARD.

FORBES: … Yes, I quite agree with what you say about the Nelson girl, Inspector.

A door opens.

FORBES: On the other hand, if she was in love with the fellow … (*Looking up*) Yes, what is it, sergeant?

SERGEANT: Mr Temple is here, sir.

FORBES: Oh, ask him in, sergeant.

SERGEANT: Very good, sir.

GERRARD: (*To FORBES: quietly*) Did you send for Temple, sir?

FORBES: No, he phoned through this morning and made an appointment.

GERRARD: Is it about this Ferguson case?

FORBES: (*Thoughtfully*) Yes, I rather imagine it is.

SERGEANT: (*Announcing*) Mr Temple, sir.

TEMPLE: Hello, Sir Graham! Good afternoon, Inspector!

GERRARD: Good afternoon.

FORBES: Well, well, you look fit, Temple. Did you have a successful trip?

TEMPLE: Yes, very, thank you.

FORBES: How's Steve?

TEMPLE: Well, at the moment she can't make up her mind whether she's in London or New York.

FORBES: I'm not surprised. Sit down.

TEMPLE: Thanks.

A moment.

FORBES: The Inspector tells me that you flew over from New York with a Mr and Mrs Ferguson.

TEMPLE: Yes, that's right, we did.

FORBES: Their son was –

TEMPLE: Yes, I know. Look, Sir Graham, it's no good beating about the bush. I'm interested in this Ferguson case, that's why I'm here.

FORBES: Well, what can we do for you, Temple?

TEMPLE: Well – so far I know very little about the case. I'd like to know exactly what happened.

GERRARD: (*Significantly*) Yes, that's what we'd like to know – exactly what happened.

TEMPLE: Well, let me have the facts: assume I know nothing whatsoever about the case.

GERRARD: Well, Richard Ferguson was a student at Oxford – Magdalen College. Although he hadn't a large circle of friends he appears to have been reasonably popular and – so far as we can gather – had no enemies. He lived in a self-contained flat which was actually the top floor of a house in Mortimer Close …

FORBES: Mortimer Close is in a residential part of Oxford, it's about a mile and a half from the College.

TEMPLE: Yes, I know. Go on, Inspector.

GERRARD: The house belongs to a Mrs Gulliver. Well, on the night of the murder, Mrs Gulliver went out to the pictures and met Richard just as she was leaving the house. According to Mrs Gulliver the boy seemed nervous and ill at ease and he told her that he had a dinner date for eight o'clock with a girl called Dinah Nelson. Well, to cut a long story short, Richard didn't keep that date. Miss Nelson waited from eight o'clock until approximately a quarter past nine.

TEMPLE: Go on …

GERRARD: Mrs Gulliver returned from the pictures just after ten: she heard no noise from the flat and

9

	she assumed Richard was still out with the girl friend. The next morning, about half past seven, she took up his usual cup of tea. (*Quietly; aside*) Have you got the photograph, Sir Graham?
FORBES:	Yes, here it is.
GERRARD:	When Mrs Gulliver opened the bedroom door, Temple … (*Passing the photograph*) this … is what … she … saw …

A moment.

TEMPLE:	Good God!
GERRARD:	The boy was on the floor near the bed: he must have been shot at very close quarters because as you can see one side of his face was almost completely blown away …
TEMPLE:	Yes. (*A pause*) Who identified the body?
FORBES:	Mrs Gulliver, Dinah Nelson, and another friend of young Ferguson's called Mrs Russell. However, just to be on the safe side we made fingerprint tests of the dead man. The prints checked all right, they were Ferguson's.
TEMPLE:	M'm. (*A moment*) Have you any idea of the time of the murder?
FORBES:	The medical people won't commit themselves. It might have been anytime between seven – when Mrs Gulliver saw him – and midnight.
TEMPLE:	What about a motive?
GERRARD:	That's just the point: there doesn't appear to be a motive.
TEMPLE:	Was anything missing?
GERRARD:	Yes, a ring. Richard used to wear it on his little finger.
FORBES:	Yes, but I doubt if the boy was murdered for a gold ring.

10

GERRARD: It seems hardly likely, sir. There was a wallet in one of the drawers with twenty odd pounds in it.

TEMPLE: Yes?

GERRARD: Well, I'm afraid that's about all.

FORBES: There was the postcard.

GERRARD: Yes, but I doubt if that's really got anything to do with the case, sir. (*To TEMPLE*) The morning Mrs Gulliver discovered the body one or two letters arrived for Richard, and a post card from Harrogate which read – "Having a wonderful time, Regards, Jonathan".

FORBES: We checked up on the card just in case Jonathan, whoever he might be, was trying to establish an alibi. But none of Richard's friends seem to have heard of anyone called Jonathan.

TEMPLE: I see. (*After a moment: suddenly*) Well, now I'd better tell you what happened last night, Sir Graham. Ferguson phoned me about half past six and asked Steve and me to go round to their hotel. He sounded pretty excited and when we got to the hotel, he gave me a copy of a magazine called The New Feature. (*He feels in his pocket*) Here it is.

FORBES: The New Feature?

TEMPLE: Yes, it's a high-brow periodical.

FORBES: Go on …

TEMPLE: Well, the magazine, marked 'Private' and addressed to Mr and Mrs Ferguson, was at the hotel when the Fergusons arrived. On page 14 there's an article on the international situation by a writer called Europa. You'll notice that someone has underlined the name Europa and scribbled a footnote.

11

FORBES: (*Examining the magazine*) Yes …

TEMPLE: Do you see what it says?

GERRARD: (*Reading*) "If you want to know who murdered your son ask Europa".

FORBES: Is this meant to be a joke?

GERRARD: Well, if it is, it's in very bad taste.

TEMPLE: No, it's not a joke.

FORBES: Well, who is Europa? It's obviously a nom de plume.

TEMPLE: It's a nom de plume all right, but, well, Ferguson showed me the magazine and asked me to find out who Europa was. He also asked me – or rather his wife did – if I would investigate the case. I said I would. (*Continuing his story*) We stayed talking until about half past ten and then Steve and I left the hotel – by the Embankment entrance – and strolled down, past the gardens, to the spot where I'd parked the car … but to my surprise someone was sitting in it.

COMPLETE FADE.

FADE UP the opening of a car door.

TEMPLE: Excuse me, but haven't you made a mistake?

DINAH: (*Tensely: she is in her middle twenties; well educated*) Oh, Mr Temple?

TEMPLE: Yes?

DINAH: Please forgive me for sitting in your car, but I did want to see you and I was afraid that I might miss you.

TEMPLE: I see. But …

DINAH: I'm Dinah Nelson. I was a friend of Richard Ferguson's.

STEVE: But what are you doing here – in our car?

DINAH: (*Obviously under an emotional strain*) I wanted to talk to Mr and Mrs Ferguson. I was just going into the hotel when I saw you and Mr Temple drive up. It was in the evening paper that you flew over from New York with the Fergusons and …

TEMPLE: Wait a minute, Miss Nelson! You get in the back, Steve. I'll sit in front with Miss Nelson.

We hear the opening of the car door.

STEVE: Yes, all right, dear.

The closing of the car door.

STEVE: Now suppose you take a deep breath and start at the beginning.

DINAH: (*Relieved by STEVE's attitude*) Thank you, Mrs Temple. (*A moment*) I was very friendly with Richard Ferguson – about eighteen months ago we became unofficially engaged. For about a year we were terribly happy together; and then, quite suddenly, Richard's attitude changed towards me.

TEMPLE: How do you mean – changed?

DINAH: Well – he used to write, you know. He wanted to be a writer, and … He suddenly got awfully cynical and bitter about things. He started criticising me; he started to compare me with a woman called Mavis Russell.

STEVE: Who's she?

DINAH: She was a friend of Richard's; a writer. She's friendly with quite a lot of the students. Her real name is Mavis Russell but she writes under the name of Europa.

TEMPLE: Does she? Does she, by Timothy! Go on, Miss Nelson.

13

DINAH: Well, to be quite candid, I don't like Mrs Russell. I never have liked her. I suppose I was jealous of her, but Mr Temple, I think she had an evil influence over Richard. I've no proof – no real proof – of what I'm saying, but … (*She hesitates*) … I think that, directly or indirectly, she was responsible for his murder.

STEVE: Is that why you wanted to see the Fergusons – to tell them about Mrs Russell?

DINAH: Yes.

TEMPLE: Have you told the police what you think?

DINAH: Yes. I saw Inspector Gerrard last night but all he did was ask me a lot of silly questions about someone I'd never even heard of – someone called Jonathan.

STEVE: Jonathan?

DINAH: Yes. Apparently this person Jonathan sent Richard a picture postcard from Harrogate or somewhere and the police can't account for it. As if it matters!

STEVE: Miss Nelson, what sort of a person is this Mrs Russell – to meet, I mean?

DINAH: Oh, charming, good looking, wealthy …

TEMPLE: When did you first meet her?

DINAH: About six months ago. My boss, Professor Dilwright, gave a cocktail party and Mrs Russell was one of the guests. I introduced her to Richard.

STEVE: Is that the Professor Dilwright, the famous historian?

DINAH: Yes, I'm his private secretary. It sounds very important, doesn't it? Actually I type chiefly very dull memos about very dull people.

STEVE: Miss Nelson, tell me – did you send a copy of the magazine The New Feature to Mr Ferguson?

DINAH: (*Surprised*) The New Feature? No! Why do you ask?

STEVE: Because someone did – with an interesting footnote about Europa alias Mrs Russell.

DINAH: Well, it wasn't me, Mrs Temple. It wasn't me …

TEMPLE: Then you're not the only person who doesn't like Mrs Russell.

FADE SCENE.

FADE UP of PAUL TEMPLE.

TEMPLE: … Well, that's what happened last night, Sir Graham. After our talk Miss Nelson decided that she couldn't face the Fergusons so we took her home. She's staying with a married sister – a Mrs Mackintosh – for two or three days.

GERRARD: My dear Temple, it's perfectly obvious that Miss Nelson sent Ferguson the magazine and that her theory about Mrs Russell is pure imagination.

TEMPLE: Most theories are imagination, Inspector. Have you seen Mrs Russell?

GERRARD: Yes, I have and she's a very charming woman.

TEMPLE: No doubt.

FORBES: Temple, do you remember an old friend of yours called Red Harris?

TEMPLE: Yes, of course – but I'd hardly call him an old friend.

FORBES: Well, you did him a favour: a very big favour, remember.

TEMPLE:	That was a long time ago. I provided the evidence that proved he was innocent – that's all. But why mention Red Harris?
FORBES:	Red spent three days in Oxford last week. He was there the night young Ferguson was murdered.
TEMPLE:	Oh! Have you spoken to him?
FORBES:	Yes. Oh, he's got an alibi: a very good one. (*Significantly*) But – I thought I'd mention it, Temple.

A moment.

GERRARD:	(*Rising*) Well, I'll take this magazine down to Rogers and get a report on the handwriting, sir.
FORBES:	Yes, all right, Inspector.
GERRARD:	Er – Temple …
TEMPLE:	Yes?
GERRARD:	If you don't think Miss Nelson sent this magazine to Ferguson, then – who do you think sent it?
TEMPLE:	Your guess is as good as mine, Inspector.
GERRARD:	Yes – but what is your guess?
TEMPLE:	Well – it might have been Mrs Russell.
GERRARD:	Mrs Russell! But good heavens, man, she wouldn't throw suspicion on to herself!
TEMPLE:	(*Smiling*) Wouldn't she? It has been done, Inspector …

FADE UP of music.

FADE DOWN of music.
We hear the sound of the flat buzzer.
The door opens.

TEMPLE:	Hello, Steve! Sorry I'm late! (*He takes off his overcoat*)

STEVE: I'll take your coat, darling. Did you see Sir Graham?

TEMPLE: Yes, I've only just left the Yard. Is there someone in the drawing room?

STEVE: Yes, it's a Mr Mackintosh. I told him you were out but he insisted on waiting.

TEMPLE: Mackintosh?

STEVE: Yes, he's some relation to Dinah Nelson.

TEMPLE: How long has he been waiting?

STEVE: Only two or three minutes.

TEMPLE: All right, let's see what it's all about.

A door opens.

REGGIE: (*A pleasant young man: he speaks with a Scots accent*) Oh, good evening, Mr Temple.

TEMPLE: Good evening.

REGGIE: My name is Mackintosh – Reggie Mackintosh.

TEMPLE: What can I do for you, Mr Mackintosh?

REGGIE: Well, I understand you saw my sister-in-law last night, Mr Temple – Dinah Nelson?

TEMPLE: That's right.

REGGIE: She's a remarkable girl, is Dinah – remarkable. And a very nice girl too when you get to know her.

TEMPLE: Yes, I'm quite sure she is.

REGGIE: Well, I suppose you're a very busy man, Mr Temple, so I'd better come straight to the point. Dinah was very friendly with Richard Ferguson, the young man that was murdered.

TEMPLE: Yes, so she told me.

REGGIE: Did she tell you that the police asked her a lot of questions about a postcard – a card that was supposed to have been sent to young Ferguson by a friend of his called Jonathan?

TEMPLE: She did mention it – yes.

17

REGGIE: Well, now, a rather curious thing has happened, Mr Temple. Whether it's of any importance or not, I wouldn't like to say, but –

TEMPLE: Well?

REGGIE: When I went down to breakfast this morning the post had already arrived and there was this postcard in the letterbox. (*He hands over the card*) You can see for yourself, it's addressed to Dinah and was posted in Harrogate.

TEMPLE: (*Reading*) "Having a wonderful time, Regards, Jonathan".

STEVE: But that's exactly what was on the other card, Paul!

REGGIE: Exactly, Mrs Temple!

STEVE: But your sister-in-law – Miss Nelson – said that she'd never heard of anyone called Jonathan.

REGGIE: I know!

STEVE: But what did she say when you showed her this postcard?

REGGIE: I – haven't shown it to her.

STEVE: You haven't!

REGGIE: No …

TEMPLE: Why not?

REGGIE: Well – Dinah's a strange girl, Mr Temple. She's highly strung, emotional, and I thought that if she saw this card she'd think that the police suspect that she had something to do with this dreadful business.

TEMPLE: Do you think she did have anything to do with it?

REGGIE: No, of course not! Dinah wouldn't harm a fly. Besides, she was in love with Richard Ferguson; you don't murder the person you're in love with.

STEVE: It has been known, Mr Mackintosh.

TEMPLE: Mackintosh, tell me; was Richard a friend of yours too?

REGGIE: No; I don't suppose I met him more than half a dozen times. My wife and I used to go up to Oxford occasionally to see Dinah and naturally we bumped into Richard.

TEMPLE: Did you like him?

REGGIE: Yes, I did. He was a pleasant chap, took himself a little too seriously perhaps but I can't for the life of me imagine why anyone should want to murder the poor chap.

TEMPLE: How long is Dinah staying with you?

REGGIE: Two or three days. I believe she's due back on Monday.

TEMPLE: Do many people know that she's staying with you?

REGGIE: Well, I couldn't say. She always does stay with us of course when she comes to London.

STEVE: Mr Mackintosh, on your visits to Oxford did you ever meet a woman called Mrs Russell?

REGGIE: Yes, I did. She was a friend of Richard's – she used to encourage him a lot – with his writing, I mean. I don't think Dinah's very keen on Mrs Russell.

TEMPLE: No, I rather gathered that. Well, thank you, Mr Mackintosh. I'll take care of this card for the time being.

REGGIE: I hope I did the right thing in bringing it to you.

TEMPLE: Yes, you did.

REGGIE: Goodbye, Mrs Temple.

STEVE: Goodbye!

REGGIE: I hope we'll meet again sometime.

STEVE: I hope so. I'll show you out, Mr Mackintosh.

REGGIE: Oh, thank you. Goodbye, Mr Temple.

TEMPLE: Goodbye!

TEMPLE lifts up the telephone receiver and commences to dial a number.

STEVE returns.

STEVE: Who are you ringing, Paul?

TEMPLE: I'm trying to get hold of a man called Red Harris. Do you remember him, Steve? We met him about six years ago.

STEVE: A tall man with a thin moustache?

TEMPLE: That's right.

STEVE: Why do you want to talk to Harris?

The number starts to ring out at the other end of the line.

TEMPLE: Sir Graham seems to think that he's mixed up in this business so I thought I might as well … (*Suddenly*) Steve, you take the phone! Ask for Harris – he's more likely to come to the phone if it's a girl speaking …

STEVE: (*Laughing*) Yes, all right. What's the number?

TEMPLE: Hop 5921 – it's a public house near the Elephant and Castle. I've an idea he'll be there.

The receiver is lifted at the other end.

SIMO: (*On the other end of the line; he is a very tough Cockney in his late forties*) Hello?

STEVE: Hop 5921?

SIMO: That's right.

STEVE: I want to speak to Mr Harris, please.

SIMO: (*Aggressive*) What Mr Harris? You got the wrong number, lady.

STEVE: Mr RED Harris.

SIMI: Oh, Red! Who is it calling?

STEVE: His mother.

SIMO: (*Laughing*) Are you Doris, the cute little number he's always talking about?

STEVE: What do you mean – cute little number!

SIMO: (*Laughing*) O.K. I'll get him. Hold on …

A moment.

TEMPLE: What's happening?

STEVE: He's coming …

TEMPLE: All right, Steve – I'll take it.

A pause.

RED: (*On the other end of the phone: angrily*) Doris?
            Listen – I told you not to ring me, didn't I?

TEMPLE: (*Interrupting RED; on the phone*) Hello, Red!
            How are you?

RED: (*After a moment*) Who is that? Who is it
            speaking?

TEMPLE: It's Temple. Paul Temple. Remember me?

RED: (*Bewildered*) Simo said it was Doris on the
            phone …

TEMPLE: That's right, Red – there's nothing to worry
            about. It was my wife.

RED: Oh, I see. What is it? What is it you want?

TEMPLE: Just a friendly chat. It's a long time since we
            met. It's about time we got together again, Red.

RED: Listen, I'm going straight now. I'm in the motor
            car rac – business. Second hand cars. Straight as
            a dye, Mr Temple.

TEMPLE: That's fine. I'm delighted to hear it.

RED: (*After a moment*) What is it you want?

TEMPLE: You spent two nights at Oxford this week, didn't
            you?

RED: That's right.

TEMPLE: Why?

RED: (*Angrily*) What do you mean – why? There's
            nothin' to stop me going' up to Oxford if I feel
            like it, is there? If you must know I went up on
            business. Picked up a car; a Lombard; she's a
            beauty. Only done two thousand miles …

TEMPLE: Is that the only reason you went to Oxford?

RED: Yes, of course.

TEMPLE: Really!

RED: Look here, what are you getting at?

TEMPLE: You didn't meet a young man called Richard Ferguson by any chance? (*A pause*) Well? (*A second pause*) Red, did you hear what I said?

RED: (*A quick, tense whisper*) Yes, I heard. Keep out of this Ferguson business ... Don't be a damn fool, Temple! Keep out of it!

RED replaces his receiver.

TEMPLE: Red, listen! Red ... (*A moment*) He's rung off ...

TEMPLE replaces his receiver.

STEVE: What did he say?

TEMPLE's thoughts are elsewhere.

STEVE: Paul, what did he say?

TEMPLE: He said he was going straight. He said he was in the motor car business and ... (*Suddenly*) Steve, what time is it?

STEVE: It's just gone six.

TEMPLE: Tell Charlie to get the car. I'm going to see Red Harris. I'm going to talk to him – I'll be back about nine.

FADE SCENE.

FADE UP the noise of two men playing snooker.

SIMO: You're rattled, Red! What's the matter with you tonight? You couldn't hit the side of a house!

RED: You're lucky, Simo. Dead lucky.

SIMO laughs.

RED: You always have been lucky at snooker.

RED throws down his cue.

SIMO: That's a tenner you owe me! Now pick that cue up and I'll tell you what I'll do.

SIMO picks up balls.

SIMO: I'll play you two 'undred up at billiards, see, give
          you fifty start and the winner … Looking for
          someone, mate?

TEMPLE: Yes, I'm looking for a Mr Red Harris.

SIMO: Well, you 'aven't got far to look. (*To RED*) Pal
          o' yours, Red?

RED: (*A moment*) No. (*To TEMPLE: surly*) I'm Harris.
          Who are you? What do you want?

TEMPLE: I understand you've got a car for sale – a two and
          a half litre Lombard.

RED: (*A moment*) That's right.

TEMPLE: Is that it outside, with trade plates?

RED: Yes, that's it.

TEMPLE: How many miles has it done?

RED: Two thousand – genuine.

SIMO: The owner only bought it to look at.

RED: Shut up, Simo!

TEMPLE: What are you asking for it?

RED: Seventeen fifty …

TEMPLE: Do you mind if I look at it?

RED: (*After a moment*) No. No, it's a pleasure. See you
          later, Simo!

SIMO: O.K.

SIMO continues to knock the balls about.
FADE SCENE.

FADE UP a faint background of traffic noises.

RED: (*Angrily*) Now what's the idea, Temple? I told
          you over the phone that I …

TEMPLE: (*With authority*) Get in the car! We can't talk
          here!

RED: We've nothing to talk about!

TEMPLE: Get in the car, Red!

23

A moment.

RED: (*Giving in*) O.K.

The car door opens: TEMPLE and RED get into the car.

RED: Now what is it? What's on your mind?

TEMPLE: Six years ago I did you a favour, Red …

RED: I know, and I haven't forgotten it.

TEMPLE: Do you remember what you said? You said any time you want anything, Mr Temple – anything – just ask Red Harris.

RED: (*Worried*) Yes, and I meant it. Honest I did. I'm a straight shooter, Mr Temple. I say exactly what I think.

TEMPLE: Then tell me: why did you spend two days in Oxford this week?

RED: I told you. I went there on business. I bought this car.

TEMPLE: You were in Oxford the night young Ferguson was murdered.

RED: I don't know anything about Ferguson.

TEMPLE: That's not what you told me on the phone.

RED: What do you mean?

TEMPLE: You said: keep out of this Ferguson business, Temple.

RED: (*Hesitatingly*) Did … I … say … that?

TEMPLE: You did, Mr Harris.

RED: (*Nervously*) Temple, listen. I'm a friend of yours. You did me a good turn once and I haven't forgotten it, but I don't know anything about Ferguson. I went up to Oxford to buy this car.

TEMPLE: Listen, Red. Let's get this straight. I'm not here because the police sent me. I'm here because the boy's father – Robert Ferguson – asked me to investigate this case. I'm not interested in what sort of a racket you're running, Red. I'm

24

interested in two things. Who murdered Richard Ferguson – and why.

RED: (*A little frightened*) I don't know anything about Ferguson. I'd never heard of the kid until I read about the murder.

TEMPLE: You're lying! Now listen, Red! I intend to get pretty tough over this business because I'm not going ... (*Suddenly*) Hello! What's this you've got in your pocket?

RED: Nothing.

TEMPLE: How long have you been carrying a revolver?

RED: It isn't a revolver, it's my pipe ...

TEMPLE takes hold of RED's arm and is forcefully taking the revolver out of his pocket.

RED: Leave go of my arm! Temple, leave go.

RED frees himself.

TEMPLE: What sort of a pipe is this? (*Angrily*) You stupid fool to get mixed up in this sort of thing!

RED: (*Angrily*) Give it to me! Give it back to me!

TEMPLE: Wait a minute! Is this the gun that shot Ferguson?

RED: Don't be a fool, Temple! Of course it isn't! You know darn well that murder isn't ... (*Suddenly*) Watch that car! Look out, he's got a gun!!! Get down!!!

The approaching car races past and there is the sound of a revolver shot and the sudden smashing of glass as the bullet hits the windscreen of RED's car. The car races away.

RED gives a sigh of relief and straightens himself.

TEMPLE: Did he hit you?

RED: No. It's a good job I saw him, otherwise ... he ... Let's go back in the pub, I want a drink ...

TEMPLE: Who was in that car – who fired the shot?

RED: (*Very frightened*) I – don't know.

TEMPLE: But you recognised him … You knew he was going to shoot …

RED: I don't know who it was! I tell you I don't know … I'm going back to the pub … I must have a drink, Temple.

TEMPLE: (*Stopping RED*) Red, wait a minute! You're mixed up in this Ferguson case: if you didn't murder Ferguson yourself then you know who did!

RED: (*Tensely*) Temple, listen! You once did me a favour – o.k. Now I'm doing you one. (*Grimly*) Whatever you do keep out of this Ferguson business.

TEMPLE: But I'm in it already! And if you've got any sense, Red – you'll talk. You'll talk to me now – as a friend – before it's too late.

A pause.

RED: (*Still overwrought*) I'll tell you one thing, Temple – and then we're all square. I don't owe you a favour and you don't owe me one. O.K.?

TEMPLE: (*After a moment*) O.K.

RED: (*Tensely*) They forgot the ring …

Dramatic FADE UP of music.

FADE DOWN of music.

FADE UP the noise of the flat buzzer: the door is opened almost as soon as the buzzer rings.

STEVE: Paul! Oh, thank goodness you've come!

TEMPLE: What's the matter, Steve?

STEVE: Mrs Ferguson's here – she's in a dreadful state. (*Confidentially*) Honestly, I think she's going out of her mind.

TEMPLE: But what's she doing here?

26

STEVE: She insists on seeing you. Mr Ferguson had to bring her, the poor man just didn't know what … Oh, here he is.

TEMPLE: Hello, Ferguson! What's the trouble?

ROBERT: (*Apologetically*) Temple, please believe me, I wouldn't have brought Helen here, but she absolutely insisted on seeing you.

TEMPLE: Where is she?

STEVE: She's in our bedroom, Paul. I've given her a sedative.

TEMPLE: Hadn't we better send for a doctor?

ROBERT: She won't hear of a doctor, she simply won't hear of it. It's you she wants to see. This business seems to have unbalanced her. She's imagining all sorts of things, Temple.

HELEN: (*From the near background*) That's not true, Robert!

ROBERT: Helen!

TEMPLE: (*Pleasantly*) Hello, Mrs Ferguson.

HELEN: (*Desperately*) Mr Temple, I've got to talk to you!

TEMPLE: Well – here I am!

HELEN: Robert thinks I'm imagining things. But I'm not. I swear I'm not!

TEMPLE: I'm quite sure you're not, Mrs Ferguson.

ROBERT: But you don't know what she's saying, Temple!

HELEN: But, Robert, it's true! I swear it's true! Mr Temple, I know you won't believe me – you'll think I've gone completely out of my mind, but – do you know what happened this morning?

TEMPLE: Yes, Mrs Ferguson. I know. (*A moment*) You saw your son.

Dramatic FADE UP of music.

END OF EPISODE ONE

27

EPISODE TWO

THAT GOOD OLD
INTUITION

OPEN TO:

TEMPLE: (*Pleasantly*) Hello, Mrs Ferguson.

HELEN: (*Desperately*) Mr Temple, I've got to talk to you!

TEMPLE: Well – here I am!

HELEN: Robert thinks I'm imagining things. But I'm not. I swear I'm not!

TEMPLE: I'm quite sure you're not, Mrs Ferguson.

ROBERT: But you don't know what she's saying, Temple!

HELEN: But, Robert, it's true! I swear it's true! Mr Temple, I know you won't believe me – you'll think I've gone completely out of my mind, but – do you know what happened this morning?

TEMPLE: Yes, Mrs Ferguson. I know. (*A moment*) You saw your son.

ROBERT: What! But how on earth did you know that she …

STEVE: Paul, do you know what you're saying!

HELEN: I knew it! I knew it was Richard. He's alive! Isn't he, Mr Temple?

ROBERT: (*Trying to pacify HELEN*) Helen, please! Darling, please!

HELEN: (*Overwrought*) You see, you wouldn't believe me, Robert! But Mr Temple believes me … He knows I'm telling the truth. (*Near to tears*)

TEMPLE: Now wait a minute, Mrs Ferguson! Wait a minute, please!

ROBERT: Temple, what the devil does this mean? You've got to explain.

TEMPLE: (*Firmly*) Now just a minute, please! (*Kindly*) Are you all right, Mrs Ferguson?

HELEN: Yes, I'm all right now, thanks.

TEMPLE: Well, we can't talk standing here. Let's go into the drawing room.

ROBERT: (*Approaching*) Now what's this all about, Temple? How did you know that my wife was under the impression that she'd seen Richard?

HELEN: But I did see him!

ROBERT: All right, my dear! Now let's hear what Mr Temple's got to say!

TEMPLE: Ferguson, I don't think you quite understand the position. If your wife did see Richard then I'm afraid you're facing a very difficult situation.

STEVE: How do you mean, Paul?

TEMPLE: Before I explain I want you, Mrs Ferguson, to tell us what happened this morning! And please, just because your story sounds fantastic, don't imagine that we're not going to believe you.

ROBERT: (*Quietly*) Go on, Helen.

HELEN: I've been almost frantic ever since I heard the news about Richard.

STEVE: Well, of course.

ROBERT: She spent most of last night crying, but this morning I finally persuaded her to go for a walk.

HELEN: I went downstairs with Robert and while he was getting his overcoat from the cloakroom I went outside the hotel and stood in front of the main entrance.

TEMPLE: Was this the front entrance, facing the Strand?

HELEN: Yes.

TEMPLE: Go on …

HELEN: Robert was rather a long time – there'd been some confusion over the cloakroom ticket – and I stood talking to the commissionaire. I don't remember what we were talking about. Anyhow while he was talking I suddenly looked up and there … a few yards away … standing on the opposite corner … watching me … was Richard

32

... At first I thought I was seeing things. I told myself it couldn't be Richard. It was impossible. Suddenly – and I'm sure he did this because he realised what I was thinking – he lifted his hat and twirled it round on his finger. Round and round ... It was a habit of his, he was always doing it, wasn't he, Robert?

ROBERT: (*Quietly*) Yes, darling.

HELEN: I stood transfixed. After a moment he replaced his hat, turned round and disappeared into the Strand. I just didn't know what to do. When Robert came I told him what had happened and – of course – he ... didn't believe me, but it <u>was</u> Richard!

TEMPLE: Ferguson, did you ask the commissionaire whether he'd seen the young man?

ROBERT: Oh – he saw a young man all right, but Temple, how could it have been Richard? I saw Richard this morning! I identified the body!

TEMPLE: Did you actually identify the body, Mr Ferguson?

ROBERT: (*Puzzled*) What do you mean?

TEMPLE: Now listen: before you even saw the body you were convinced that your son had been murdered. He'd already been identified by three people and by a fingerprint test. Now the point is this – and it's important, Ferguson – quite apart from what you'd been told, did you personally see any definite marks of identification?

ROBERT: (*Thoughtfully*) No. No, I didn't. Richard had no definite marks – no special peculiarities. Of course, it was impossible to identify the features because of the shot, but ...

TEMPLE: Well?

ROBERT: Well, he was the same build as Richard, the same colouring, he was dressed in one of Richard's suits, he was found in the flat.

TEMPLE: But you're not certain, are you, Ferguson? You're not one hundred per cent certain.

ROBERT: I don't know, I … Temple, do you think there really is a chance that Richard's still alive?

TEMPLE: Yes, I do. (*Confidentially*) I've just been talking to a man called Red Harris. He gave me certain information, which made me suspect that your son had not been murdered. When I got home and Steve told me that Mrs Ferguson was here and almost demented, I guessed what had happened.

ROBERT: But Temple, if Richard isn't dead then who was murdered?

TEMPLE: What a minute! A few moments ago I told you that you were facing a very difficult situation. Believe me, I didn't exaggerate.

STEVE: I think I know what that situation is.

HELEN: What do you mean, Mrs Temple?

STEVE: If Paul is right and Richard is alive then … obviously … he's got to be found …

ROBERT: Of course!

TEMPLE: We shall need your help, Ferguson. We shall need all the help we can get.

HELEN: (*Bewildered*) But Mr Temple, don't you understand – we want to find Richard.

ROBERT: Wait a moment, Helen! I think I see what you're getting at, Temple! You think that Richard committed the murder. You think that he deliberately fostered the impression that he was the victim so that …

34

TEMPLE: The moment I convince Scotland Yard that Richard Ferguson isn't dead they'll get a warrant out for his arrest.

HELEN: I don't believe that Richard committed the murder! I just don't believe it …

ROBERT: Helen, please! Temple, our main concern is to find Richard. What action the police decide to take when we have found him – well we'll cross that bridge when we come to it. Now what can we do? How can we help you?

TEMPLE: I want you and Mrs Ferguson to go back to the hotel: during the next few days lead your normal life. Go shopping; if you've got any business appointments keep them.

HELEN: You do think Richard will get in touch with us?

TEMPLE: Well, I think there's a chance, Mrs Ferguson – a very good chance.

ROBERT: And if he does?

TEMPLE: Phone me immediately, or Inspector Gerrard.

The door opens.

CHARLIE: Excuse me, sir.

TEMPLE: Yes – what is it, Charlie?

CHARLIE: Sir Graham Forbes is here, sir. I've put him in the study.

TEMPLE: Thank you, Charlie.

STEVE: Did you ask Sir Graham to call?

TEMPLE: Yes, I phoned him about an hour ago. Steve, go and have a word with him. I'll be with you in two or three minutes.

STEVE: Yes, all right. Goodbye, Mrs Ferguson – and try not to worry too much.

HELEN: Thank you. I feel now that there's a chance that everything's going to be fine again!

ROBERT: I hope you're right, Helen. I certainly hope you're right.

FADE SCENE.

Slow FADE UP of SIR GRAHAM and TEMPLE. They are having a serious but quite friendly argument.

FORBES: ... Well, I'm not convinced, Temple! Just because Mrs Ferguson imagines she saw her son —

TEMPLE: (*Interrupting FORBES*) Sir Graham, listen! Harris said: "They forgot the ring". Now what do you think he meant by that? There's only one possible explanation. The ring was not stolen because it was never on the body, for the simple reason that the body was not the body of Richard Ferguson.

STEVE: Sir Graham, you mentioned the fingerprint test. What does the test consist of?

FORBES: We took the fingerprints of the dead man and compared them with those of Richard Ferguson. They were identical.

STEVE: Had you a record of Ferguson's prints?

FORBES: No.

STEVE: Then how were you able to compare them?

FORBES: We did what we always do in a case of this kind, Steve. We tested various objects in the flat. Ferguson's cigarette case, his razor, his wallet, his hairbrush, and so on. His fingerprints were on every one of them – they were the fingerprints of the dead man.

TEMPLE: I don't question that, Sir Graham! I simply question whether the dead man was Richard Ferguson!

FORBES: Look here, Temple, what you are trying to say is this! Someone was murdered, taken to Richard Ferguson's flat and dressed in his clothes. The people responsible then proceeded to plant the fingerprints of the murdered man on Richard's personal effects knowing full well …

TEMPLE: Knowing full well that you would test Richard's personal effects in order to get a sample of his fingerprints. You haven't got Richard Ferguson's fingerprints, you've only got the fingerprints of the dead man!

FORBES: I can hardly believe that, Temple! Now look, if the murdered man isn't Richard Ferguson then who is he and why was he murdered?

TEMPLE: Well, if it comes to that, why was Richard Ferguson murdered?

STEVE: Supposing you're right, Paul, and what you say actually did happen. Then this person – the person that committed the murder – must be very thorough.

TEMPLE: But of course he's thorough!

STEVE: Then why did he forget the signet ring? Even if he hadn't Richard's ring you'd have thought he'd have substituted one.

FORBES: Let's assume that before young Ferguson was shot he put up a pretty good fight and during the course of the fight the signet ring came off. The people – or person – responsible for the murder then tidied the room but forgot the signet ring. That's what Red Harris meant.

TEMPLE: I don't agree. When Harris said "They forgot the ring" he said it with a particular significance. In any case, Sir Graham, you can't ignore the fact that Mrs Ferguson saw Richard.

FORBES: Nonsense! An hallucination! The woman's overwrought and highly strung. In my opinion she saw a young man who looked like Richard and being in a nervy state … (*He stops, interrupted by the sudden opening of the door*)

Sudden opening of the door.

STEVE: (*Annoyed*) Yes – what is it, Charlie?

CHARLIE: (*Harassed*) I'm awfully sorry, Mrs Temple, but a Mr Mackintosh is 'ere and insists on seeing Mr Temple. I told him you was engaged but he won't listen.

REGGIE: (*Bursting in, excited*) Mr Temple. I'm sorry, but I must speak to you.

TEMPLE: This is Sir Graham Forbes, Mr Mackintosh.

REGGIE: (*Still excited*) Yes, we've met. (*Tensely*) Mr Temple, there's something I've got to tell you. It's important – terribly important.

TEMPLE: Well?

REGGIE: This afternoon my sister-in-law – Dinah Nelson – had a telephone call from her boss – Professor Dilwright – telling her to report back to Oxford first thing tomorrow morning.

TEMPLE: Well …

REGGIE: Well, I've just taken Dinah to the station. I put her on the train and then went down to the underground. As I got onto the platform there was a train leaving and I noticed a young fellow standing by one of the doors. (*Excited*) Mr Temple, I only caught a glimpse of him, but – I'll swear I'm not mistaken! It was Richard Ferguson.

A slight pause.

TEMPLE: Is this another hallucination, Sir Graham?

FADE UP of music.

FADE DOWN of music.

STEVE: Would you like some more coffee, Paul?

TEMPLE: Yes, thank you, darling. It's very good coffee, Steve – where did you get it?

STEVE: New York. I brought it back with us.

TEMPLE: I thought so. It's got a distinct taste of nylon.

STEVE: (*Laughing*) Here you are!

TEMPLE: Thanks.

STEVE: I'm glad we didn't make a date tonight.

TEMPLE: Yes, so am I.

STEVE: (*Making herself comfortable*) It's nice to be home again. (*A moment*) What happened this afternoon?

TEMPLE: Well, I saw Sir Graham and Inspector Gerrard. We had a chat with our Scots friend – Reggie Mackintosh. The Inspector took a sample of his handwriting.

STEVE: What did he do that for?

TEMPLE: He wanted to compare it with the handwriting on the magazine The New Feature – the one that was sent to Ferguson.

STEVE: Was it the same?

TEMPLE: No.

STEVE: Mackintosh seemed pretty excited last night, didn't he? Bursting in like that!

TEMPLE: Well, wouldn't you be excited if you saw someone you thought was dead! Anyhow, he convinced Sir Graham.

STEVE: Paul, what do you think really happened? Do you think young Ferguson did commit the murder and then deliberately faked things?

TEMPLE: I don't know, Steve. I was talking to Gerrard this afternoon about those postcards – the one that was meant for Richard and the one that Dinah

39

	Nelson received, or would have received if it hadn't been for Mackintosh.
STEVE:	You mean the ones from Jonathan?
TEMPLE:	Yes. I had a hunch that the person who posted the cards also sent Ferguson the magazine. It wasn't a very good hunch I'm afraid – the handwriting's quite different.
STEVE:	Paul …
TEMPLE:	Yes?
STEVE:	Now don't laugh …
TEMPLE:	What do you mean – don't laugh?
STEVE:	I've got a sort of intuition.
TEMPLE:	(*Laughing*) Oh, by Timothy, not that good old intuition, Steve!
STEVE:	No, really, darling. I'm serious.
TEMPLE:	Well, come on, let's have it.
STEVE:	Do you know what I think? I think Reggie Mackintosh was lying last night. I don't think he did see Richard Ferguson.
TEMPLE:	You mean – you don't think that young Ferguson is alive?
STEVE:	No! I think he's alive. I think Mrs Ferguson saw him, but – I don't think Reggie Mackintosh did.
TEMPLE:	Well, if he didn't see him what on earth was the point of saying that he did?
STEVE:	(*Laughing*) I don't know, darling. My intuition doesn't work that fast.
TEMPLE:	I'm not so sure that it works at all! Give me a cigarette.
STEVE:	There's a box beside you.
TEMPLE:	Oh, yes.
STEVE:	Do you know what I did this afternoon while you were at Scotland Yard?
TEMPLE:	No.

STEVE: I read a book.

TEMPLE: Well – I hope you enjoyed it.

STEVE: I wouldn't say I enjoyed it. I found it interesting. It was called The Purple Moon.

TEMPLE: Well?

STEVE: … by Mavis Russell.

TEMPLE: (*Intrigued*) Really?

STEVE: Yes, I thought you'd be interested. Paul, I think you ought to make a point of meeting Mrs Russell. I'm not so sure, after reading her book, that Dinah Nelson wasn't telling the truth.

TEMPLE: What do you mean?

STEVE: I think Mavis Russell might quite easily be the sort of person who could have an evil influence on an impressionable young man.

TEMPLE: The book certainly seems to have impressed you, darling! As a matter of fact I agree about Mrs Russell. It might be a very good idea if we went up to Oxford for two or three days.

The telephone rings.

TEMPLE: Now who can this be?

TEMPLE lifts the receiver on the phone.

TEMPLE: Hello?

ROBERT: (*On the other end of the line*) Hello? Is that you, Temple?

TEMPLE: Yes – who is that?

ROBERT: This is Robert Ferguson …

TEMPLE: Oh, good evening.

ROBERT: (*Quietly, almost as if he is afraid of being overheard*) Temple, I've got some news … I've got to be quick because I don't want Helen to overhear me …

TEMPLE: What is it?

ROBERT: (*Hesitantly*) I've – heard – from Richard …

41

TEMPLE: (*Quickly*) When?

ROBERT: (*Worried*) About half an hour ago. He telephoned me ... Temple, please don't tell the police ... Don't say anything, not yet ...

TEMPLE: What's the matter?

ROBERT: I think he's in trouble. He needs money, he ... asked ... me to meet him ...

TEMPLE: When? Tonight?

ROBERT: Yes ...

TEMPLE: Where?

ROBERT: (*Worried*) Temple, I can't tell you, not over the phone, I ... (*Hesitantly, tense*) Can – can you pick me up in about twenty minutes?

TEMPLE: Yes. Where are you now?

ROBERT: I'm at the hotel. Meet me at the back entrance, facing the Embankment – bring your car ...

TEMPLE: All right.

ROBERT: I'll explain when I see you, Temple.

TEMPLE: It's just five to ten. I'll be there by quarter past.

ROBERT: O.K. Thanks.

TEMPLE replaces his receiver.

STEVE: Who was it, Paul?

TEMPLE: It was Ferguson – he's heard from Richard.

STEVE: He has!

TEMPLE: Tell Charlie to get the car, darling.

STEVE: Why? What's happening?

TEMPLE: I'm afraid we've got a date after all, Steve.

FADE UP of music.

FADE DOWN of music.

FADE UP noises of pouring rain.

FADE UP the noise of TEMPLE's car as it draws slowly to a standstill.

The rain continues.

STEVE: What a night!

TEMPLE: I can hardly see through the windscreen. Oh, there's Ferguson, by the lamp post.

STEVE: Where? Oh, yes, I don't think he's seen us. You'd better blow the horn.

TEMPLE blows the car horn.

TEMPLE: What's the matter with the fellow?

TEMPLE blows the horn again.

STEVE: He's seen us!

A moment.

ROBERT: Hello!

TEMPLE opens the car door.

FADE UP the noise of the rain.

TEMPLE: Jump in, Ferguson.

ROBERT: (*Under an obvious physical strain*) Thanks, I'm sorry, Temple, I – I did see you but I … couldn't … make … it … (*He is breathless*)

STEVE: What is it, Mr Ferguson ?

TEMPLE: What's the matter?

ROBERT: It's this old heart of mine; it lets me down every now and again. I was feeling perfectly all right … standing in the doorway … and … then … suddenly … (*He is in pain*)

TEMPLE: Would you like me to take you back to the hotel?

ROBERT: No … No, it'll pass … I'll be all right in a minute …

TEMPLE: I've got some brandy here.

ROBERT: No – no, I mustn't take it. I've got some tablets for this sort of thing but they're in the hotel. I'll be all right, Temple, don't worry …

A pause.

STEVE: As long as you are all right.

ROBERT: (*A moment*) I thought this would happen. The moment I start worrying about anything I always get this … confounded … heart … trouble …

TEMPLE: (*After a moment*) I'm sorry. Now, what happened tonight, Ferguson?

ROBERT: Richard telephoned … Fortunately Helen was in the bath … I was expecting a business call from Birmingham … When I picked up the phone and heard Richard's voice I … just couldn't believe it …

TEMPLE: What did he say?

ROBERT: He said … "I'm in trouble – terrible trouble. Please don't ask any questions and listen to what I've got to say …" He said he needed money … he asked me to take it to an address in Lewisham. I wrote it down … Here it is, Temple …

TEMPLE: Did he say anything else?

ROBERT: No. He wouldn't let me ask any questions. When I started to talk he hung up on me. He sounded desperate. If you want my opinion the boy's ill – that's why I didn't want you to contact the police – not tonight.

TEMPLE: Is this the address – 439, Galveston Road, Lewisham?

ROBERT: Yes.

STEVE: Why have you written the name Griffiths?

ROBERT: He told me to ask for Mr Griffiths. I think he must be staying there under that name.

TEMPLE: Yes, most probably. Does Mrs Ferguson know about this?

ROBERT: No, I told her it was the Birmingham call. Right now she thinks I'm in the bar drinking … double … (*In pain again*) … Oh, gee … the darned …

(*In obvious pain*) … thing … seems to have … come back … Oh!

A pause.

TEMPLE: Ferguson, listen – you can't come out to Lewisham – not like this.

ROBERT: (*Still in pain*) I'll be all right. I've had this sort of thing happen to me before.

TEMPLE: If you see your son and start getting excited you might have a very bad attack. The best thing you can do is go straight back to the hotel and go to bed.

STEVE: He's right, Mr Ferguson.

TEMPLE: We'll see Richard. We'll bring him back to the hotel – tonight – I promise.

ROBERT: You … won't take him to the police first, will you?

TEMPLE: I've told you. I'll bring him back to the hotel.

ROBERT: O.K., Temple. Thanks. (*Still in pain*) Give me your arm …

TEMPLE: Open the door, Steve.

ROBERT: (*Resting on TEMPLE's arm*) That's it … that's fine …

TEMPLE: I shan't be long, Steve.

ROBERT: I'll be o.k. once I get to the elevator.

COMPLETE FADE.

Slow FADE UP the sound of very heavy rain and the sound of TEMPLE's car which is crawling along Galveston Road. TEMPLE and STEVE are scanning the houses.

STEVE: I'm not sure that it's on this side of the road.

TEMPLE: It must be! We passed four hundred and three ages ago. (*Suddenly*) Here we are, 439.

The car slows to a standstill.

STEVE: I don't see the number.

45

TEMPLE:	It's on the gate.
STEVE:	(*Peering*) It might be anything.
TEMPLE:	Anyway, we'll try it. We'd better make a dash for it.
STEVE:	What a night! Why on earth didn't we bring an umbrella!
TEMPLE:	Be careful you don't slip.

The car door opens and closes with a bang.
FADE SCENE.

FADE UP the sound of rain in the near background.

TEMPLE:	(*Arriving, breathless*) Phew!
STEVE:	Isn't it awful! I'm drenched.
TEMPLE:	What a delightful looking establishment! I should think young Ferguson's finding this a bit of a come down!
STEVE:	Yes …

TEMPLE pulls the bell handle and inside the house an old fashioned bell can be heard ringing.

TEMPLE:	Let's try it again!

We hear the sound of the bell inside the house again.
A pause.

STEVE:	Do you think there's anyone in?
TEMPLE:	Yes, I think so – there's a light showing.

A pause.
We hear the sound of footsteps.

TEMPLE:	Someone's coming now.

The door opens.

TEMPLE:	(*Pleasantly*) Good evening …
MRS PARSONS:	(*A blousy woman in her late forties: she speaks with an artificial accent which merely emphasises her cockney*) Who is it? What do you want?

TEMPLE:	Is this four hundred and thirty-nine Galveston Road?
MRS PARSONS:	It's Santa Rosa – we don't go by numbers.
TEMPLE:	(*Pleasantly*) But it is four hundred and thirty-nine?
MRS PARSONS:	Yes – as a matter of fact it is.
TEMPLE:	We've an appointment with Mr Griffiths.
MRS PARSONS:	(*Surprised*) Oh! Is he expecting you?
TEMPLE:	Yes, I've told you. We've an appointment.
MRS PARSONS:	It's a bit late for appointments, isn't it? It's nearly 'alf past eleven.
TEMPLE:	Mr Griffiths asked us to come. It's very important.
MRS PARSONS:	(*Doubtful*) Well – I don't know, I'm sure. (*Suspiciously*) Haven't see you before, 'ave I? You're not one of the regulars.
STEVE:	(*Laughing*) Look, Mrs – ?
MRS PARSONS:	Parsons is the name …
STEVE:	Look, Mrs Parsons, we can't stand out here! The rain's pouring off your roof – it's like standing under a waterfall.
MRS PARSONS:	Well – you'd better come in.
TEMPLE:	Thank you.

TEMPLE and STEVE enter the house and the door is closed behind them.

MRS PARSONS:	I told Mr Griffiths when he took the room. I said no visitors after ten o'clock. If he can't do what he wants to do before ten o'clock it's a poor look out. Still, I suppose you've got to make an exception on a night like this. You'll find Mr Griffiths in his room – it's the door at the top of the stairs.
TEMPLE:	Thank you.

MRS PARSONS: Wait a minute, I'll put the light on! Just 'ark at that rain! It's a terrible night, isn't it? It took me an hour an' three quarters to get back from Walham Green. An hour an' three quarters. I told my sister, I'll never do it again. Never.

TEMPLE: Is that the room – up there?

MRS PARSONS: Yes, but perhaps you'd better wait down 'ere. I'll pop up an' tell him you've arrived. He's a bit on the funny side is Mr Griffiths.

TEMPLE: Thank you.

MRS PARSONS ascends the stairs.

After a pause we hear her knocking on the bedroom door.

MRS PARSONS: Mr Griffiths! Mr Griffiths, your friends are here! Mr Griffiths!

We hear the sound of the bedroom room opening.

A moment.

We then hear a loud hysterical scream from MRS PARSONS.

STEVE: Paul!

TEMPLE: Come on, Steve! Quickly!

FADE SCENE.

Quick FADE UP.

MRS PARSONS: (*Crying and almost hysterical*) He's dead … Dead! … There's blood all over the floor … Oh, my God, what's happened! What's happened!?

TEMPLE: Stay here, Steve, with Mrs Parsons. I'm going into the bedroom.

MRS PARSONS: He's dead … I saw him, as soon as I opened the door … (*Near hysterical*) I could see the body near the bed … There's blood all over the carpet … There's blood

48

everywhere … This is terrible! What will people say? What will they say? (*She continues crying*)

The bedroom door closes.

STEVE:	Is he dead?
TEMPLE:	Yes … (*With quiet authority*) Mrs Parsons, that man in there – the man that's been murdered. Is that Mr Griffiths?
MRS PARSONS:	(*Surprised*) Why, yes! Yes, of course it is! You know it's Mr Griffiths!
STEVE:	Paul, what is it?
TEMPLE:	(*A moment*) It's not young Ferguson. It's Red Harris.

FADE UP of music.

FADE DOWN of music.
Slow FADE UP of a telephone ringing.
It rings for some time then suddenly the receiver is lifted.

TEMPLE:	(*On the phone, breathlessly*) Hello?
FORBES:	(*On the other end of the phone*) Hello – is that you, Temple?
TEMPLE:	(*Trying to regain his breath*) Oh, hello, Sir Graham! You've only just caught us! We were halfway down the stairs …
FORBES:	Where are you off to – Oxford?
TEMPLE:	Yes. How did you guess?
FORBES:	The Inspector told me; he said he thought you'd probably be going up there for two or three days.
TEMPLE:	Yes. I want to meet Mrs Russell and one or two of the University people.
FORBES:	I'll phone Max Wyman and tell him to look you up.

TEMPLE:	Max Wyman? Is he the young fellow who wrote a biography of Marcus Aurelius?
FORBES:	Yes, that's right. He's Lord Elsworth's youngest son – he's at Balliol. He knows pretty well everybody in Oxford. If you want an introduction to anybody he's your man.
TEMPLE:	I'll be glad to meet him. Sir Graham, tell me; did the Inspector see Ferguson?
FORBES:	Yes, and the old boy's convinced – absolutely convinced – that it was Richard that spoke to him on the phone.
TEMPLE:	And what about Red Harris?
FORBES:	Our people think the murder was committed at about half past nine – which would be about an hour and a half before you got there and about an hour before Mrs Parsons got back from Walham Green.
TEMPLE:	I see. How long had he been staying at the house?
FORBES:	He checked in on Monday and paid a week's rent in advance; incidentally, he'd been using the name Griffiths for some time. He had a driving licence in that name.
TEMPLE:	I see. (*Suddenly*) Well, I'll contact you when I get back from Oxford, Sir Graham.
FORBES:	All right, Temple. I'll phone Wyman this afternoon.
TEMPLE:	Thanks. Goodbye!
FORBES:	Goodbye, Temple!

The receiver is replaced.
FADE UP of music.

FADE DOWN of music.

STEVE: Where would you like me to put these shirts, Paul?

TEMPLE: In the wardrobe.

STEVE: There isn't any more room in the wardrobe. I'd better put them in the chest of drawers.

TEMPLE: What do you mean – there isn't any more room in the wardrobe? (*Curious*) How many dresses have you brought down here?

TEMPLE opens the wardrobe door.

TEMPLE: By Timothy, Steve! You really are the limit! This is Oxford not the South of France!

STEVE: You can't expect the wife of a successful novelist to go around looking like a tramp.

TEMPLE: Come off it! I've got wise to that one!

The telephone rings.

TEMPLE: (*On the phone*) Hello?

PORTER: (*On the other end of an internal line*) Mr Temple?

TEMPLE: Yes …

PORTER: This is the Hall Porter speaking. There's a gentleman to see you, sir. A Mr Wyman.

TEMPLE: Oh, send him up, please.

PORTER: Very good, sir.

TEMPLE replaces the receiver.

TEMPLE: It's Sir Graham's friend – Max Wyman.

STEVE: Oh. (*Pulling on her dress*) Give me a hand with this dress, darling.

TEMPLE: (*Getting hold of the dress*) Keep your head down!

STEVE: Careful or you'll tear it! (*Struggling into the dress*) I suppose you'd better invite Wyman to dinner. He'll probably be a very useful contact while we're down here.

TEMPLE: Yes.

STEVE: Zip me up the back, darling.

TEMPLE zips STEVE's dress.

TEMPLE: I wonder if Wyman knows Mrs Russell?

STEVE: Didn't Sir Graham say he was Lord Elsworth's son?

TEMPLE: Yes.

STEVE: Then he knows Mrs Russell! She'll have seen to that all right!

TEMPLE: (*Laughing*) Yes, I expect so.

There is a knock on the door.

STEVE: Here he is.

TEMPLE opens the door.

TEMPLE: (*Pleasantly*) Come in, Mr Wyman.

WYMAN: (*Well spoken, pleasant, in the middle twenties*) Sir Graham phoned me, Mr Temple. He said you were staying down here for two or three days and he asked me to look you up.

TEMPLE closes the door.

TEMPLE: That's very nice of you. This is my wife. Steve, this is Mr Wyman.

STEVE: How do you do?

WYMAN: How do you do?

WYMAN: You probably think it's odd my dropping in on you quite so soon but Sir Graham said you were rather anxious to meet Mrs Russell.

TEMPLE: Yes, as a matter of fact I am. I understand she was a very close friend of young Ferguson's.

STEVE: How long have you known Mrs Russell?

WYMAN: Oh – two or three years. At one time we saw rather a lot of each other. She thought of writing a book on Justinian I, you know – the Roman Emperor – the fellow who bumped off that blighter Phocas.

TEMPLE laughs.

WYMAN: I'm supposed to be rather bright on that
            particular period so dear Mavis picked my
            brains for a month or so – she's a jolly good
            picker too when she gets going.
TEMPLE: Did she write the book?
WYMAN: No, she didn't. She changed her mind and
            wrote an absolute shocker called The Purple
            Moon.
STEVE: (*Laughing*) Mr Wyman, you're a man after my
            own heart!
WYMAN: Have you read it?
STEVE: Yes.
WYMAN: Isn't it awful? Ye Gods, what a woman! Give
            me La Vie Parisienne every time.

They all laugh.

WYMAN: Anyhow, to get to the point. Mavis is giving a
            cocktail party – tonight – at seven o'clock.
            She's invited me and a girl friend.
TEMPLE: Well?
WYMAN: (*Amused*) Well – I thought it might be a very
            good idea if Mrs Temple turned out to be the
            girl friend.
TEMPLE: A very good idea!
WYMAN: Then later on Mrs Temple can introduce you to
            Mrs Russell. It strikes me as a much better idea
            than you just – sort of – barging in on her.
TEMPLE: Yes, I agree. What about it, Steve?
STEVE: I'm game.
WYMAN: Well, in that case I think we ought to be
            making a move. It's nearly seven o'clock now.
TEMPLE: What time will you be back?
WYMAN: Oh, half past eight at the latest. I'll drop Mrs
            Temple at the hotel.

53

TEMPLE:	No, don't do that. Let's all have dinner together – say quarter to nine.
WYMAN:	Thanks.
TEMPLE:	By the way, I expect you know Dinah Nelson?
WYMAN:	Oh, very well! Now she <u>was</u> a close friend of Richard's.
TEMPLE:	Miss Nelson is under the impression that Mrs Russell exercised a sort of evil influence over him.
WYMAN:	It all depends what you mean by an evil influence. Richard was very impressed by her but he was rather an impressionable young man.
TEMPLE:	Are you impressed by her?
WYMAN:	Not in quite the same way. (*Pleasantly*) Are you ready, Mrs Temple?
STEVE:	Yes – and you'd better make it Steve!
WYMAN:	(*Laughing*) Yes, I think I'd better, Mrs Temple – Steve.

They all laugh.

| TEMPLE: | Tell the Hall Porter to send up the evening paper, darling. Don't forget. |
| STEVE: | Yes, all right, Paul. |

FADE SCENE.

Quick FADE UP background conversation of the hotel lounge.

STEVE:	Excuse me, Mr Wyman – I shan't be a moment. I'm just going to have a word with the Hall Porter.
WYMAN:	Right. I'll get the car. See you outside.
STEVE:	Yes.

STEVE crosses to the desk.

STEVE:	Would you send an evening paper up to Room 175, please? And tomorrow morning …
PORTER:	Mrs Temple?
STEVE:	Yes.
PORTER:	You're wanted on the telephone, madam. Will you take it over here, please?
STEVE:	Oh, yes, of course.
PORTER:	(*A moment*) Here you are, madam.
STEVE:	Thank you. Oh! Hello, Mr Wyman. Didn't you get the car?
WYM AN:	No, I thought I'd wait for you.
STEVE:	Excuse me a moment. I'm wanted on the phone.
WYMAN:	Yes, of course.
STEVE:	(*On the phone*) Hello?
TEMPLE:	Steve, where are you speaking from?
STEVE:	I'm in the hall.
TEMPLE:	In a box?
STEVE:	No.
TEMPLE:	Are you alone?
STEVE:	No.
TEMPLE:	Is Wyman with you?
STEVE:	Yes.
TEMPLE:	Can he overhear what I'm saying?
STEVE:	I don't think so.
TEMPLE:	Listen, Steve. That man's an imposter. He isn't Max Wyman!

FADE UP of music.

END OF EPISODE TWO

EPISODE THREE

THE RING

OPEN TO:

TEMPLE: (*On the phone*) Listen, Steve. That man's an imposter. He isn't Max Wyman!

STEVE: Oh … (*A pause – quite gay*) Really? What an extraordinary thing!

TEMPLE: You heard what I said?

STEVE: Yes.

TEMPLE: Is he still standing near you?

STEVE: M'm – fairly.

TEMPLE: Now listen … Go outside – walk up to the car with him, and then suddenly pretend that you've left your handbag in the bedroom and come back to the hotel. I'll see you in the hall.

STEVE: Yes. All right.

TEMPLE: Oh, and get the number of the car.

STEVE: Yes, do that. Look forward to seeing you. Goodbye.

STEVE replaces the receiver.

WYMAN: Ready now?

STEVE: Yes, quite ready, Mr Wyman.

WYMAN: Oh, you've left your handbag.

STEVE: Oh – thank you.

As WYMAN and STEVE walk across the hall:

WYMAN: Was that your husband on the phone?

STEVE: No. It was an old girl friend of mine.

WYMAN: It didn't sound like a girl friend.

STEVE: It's the sort of "girl friend" I'd rather you didn't mention to my husband.

WYMAN: Oh. (*A laugh*) Oh, I see.

STEVE: I hope you do see, Mr Wyman. Where's your car?

WYMAN: It's just round the corner.

FADE SCENE.

FADE UP street noises.

STEVE: This is rather a dashing car. What is it?

WYMAN: It's a new Phoenix.

STEVE: Is it jet-propelled?

WYMAN: It's not as fast as it looks. Jump in.

STEVE: If I'm going to ride in this chariot I'll need a scarf.

WYMAN: Nonsense. You don't need a scarf.

STEVE: (*Going*) I certainly do. I shan't be a minute, Mr Wyman.

WYMAN: (*To himself*) I bet you won't – blast you.

FADE SCENE.

FADE UP STEVE entering the hotel.

TEMPLE: All right, Steve?

STEVE: Yes.

TEMPLE: Where is he – in the car?

STEVE: Yes, but I think he suspects something. I left my handbag on the desk and he spotted it …

TEMPLE: Where is the car?

STEVE: Just round the corner.

TEMPLE: Come on then.

FADE SCENE.

FADE UP of the car making a speedy departure.

TEMPLE: Yes, you were right, Steve. There he goes.

STEVE: He looked suspicious when I put the phone down.

TEMPLE: Did you get the car number?

STEVE: Yes. YEW 890.

TEMPLE: Well, thank goodness you're all right, anyway.

STEVE: But how on earth did you know he wasn't Wyman?

60

TEMPLE: The penny dropped just as you walked out. I suddenly remember what he said about Mrs Russell.

STEVE: What do you mean?

TEMPLE: He said she thought of writing a book on Justinian I, the Roman Emperor who murdered Phocas.

STEVE: Well?

TEMPLE: Well, the real Max Wyman would never have made a mistake like that. Phocas was murdered by a character called Heraclius.

STEVE: Get you! Fancy you remembering that!

TEMPLE: Yes, but I only just remembered it! Come on, let's go back to the hotel.

FADE SCENE.

FADE UP.

TEMPLE: Will you get me a call to London, please?

PORTER: Certainly, sir.

TEMPLE: Putney 9301 – a personal call to Sir Graham Forbes. It's rather urgent so try to get it through as quickly as possible.

PORTER: Very good, sir. Shall I put it through to your room, sir?

TEMPLE: Yes, please.

STEVE: Oh, by the way, that gentleman – Mr Wyman – have you ever seen him before?

PORTER: No, madam. (*Curious*) Is anything wrong? I saw you rush out of the hotel and I wondered if …

TEMPLE: No, no, it's quite all right. Try and get that call through as soon as possible.

PORTER: Right away, sir! Oh, Mr Temple, here's your evening paper!

TEMPLE: Oh, thank you. (*A pause*) By Timothy!

61

STEVE: What is it, Paul?
TEMPLE: Look at the front page! The Fleet Street boys
            have certainly gone to town!
STEVE: (*Reading*) "Is Richard Ferguson Alive?
            Mystery of University Undergraduate!"
TEMPLE: "Paul Temple in Oxford …" Someone must
            have talked. It's either one of the Fergusons or
            Reggie Mackintosh.
STEVE: Yes …
TEMPLE: Come on. Let's go up to our room …
FADE SCENE.

FADE UP STEVE.
STEVE: Paul, what do you think would have happened
            if you hadn't spotted that slip of Wyman's – or
            whatever his name was?
TEMPLE: I wonder. (*Thoughtfully*) You know, Steve, it's
            my bet that whoever's behind all this must
            think that I'm on to something.
STEVE: And tried to abduct me in order to divert your
            attention.
TEMPLE: Exactly.
STEVE: I suppose all that talk about a cocktail party at
            Mrs Russell's was nonsense?
The telephone starts ringing.
TEMPLE: Yes, of course.
STEVE: That will be your call to Sir Graham.
TEMPLE: (*On the phone*) Hello?
OPERATOR: (*On the other end of the line*) Your call to
            London, sir. Hold on a moment, please.
FORBES: (*On the other end of the line*) Hello?
OPERATOR: Is that Sir Graham Forbes speaking personally?
FORBES: Yes …
OPERATOR: Go ahead please …

TEMPLE: Hello, Sir Graham! Temple here …
FORBES: Oh, hello, Temple!
TEMPLE: Sir Graham, tell me – did you get in touch with
          Max Wyman?
FORBES: I phoned his digs soon after you left.
          Unfortunately Wyman's away, he's not due back
          in Oxford until tomorrow night.
TEMPLE: Who did you speak to?
FORBES: (*Puzzled*) What do you mean?
TEMPLE: Who did you speak to when you phoned?
FORBES: I spoke to a young fellow called Rudolf Charles.
          He said he was a roommate of Wyman's.
TEMPLE: Did you leave a message?
FORBES: Yes. I told him to tell Wyman that you were
          staying at The Star Hotel. Temple, is anything
          the matter?
TEMPLE: Yes – someone impersonated Wyman and tried
          to abduct Steve.
FORBES: What!?
TEMPLE: We got the car number – YEW 820.
FORBES: I'll get the Oxford people on to that straight
          away!
TEMPLE: Sir Graham, what did this fellow Charles sound
          like?
FORBES: He was a foreigner – rather an attractive accent.
          Seemed a pleasant sort of fellow over the phone.
          Temple, you don't think that he impersonated
          Wyman?
TEMPLE: No, no, it doesn't sound like it. (*Suddenly*) All
          right, Sir Graham. I'll keep in touch. Goodbye.
FORBES: Goodbye, Temple!

TEMPLE replaces the receiver.

TEMPLE:	Sir Graham telephoned Wyman but Wyman was away. He left a message with a man called Rudolf Charles.
STEVE:	Do you think it was Charles who impersonated Wyman?
TEMPLE:	I doubt it, that would be just a little too obvious.
STEVE:	You know, Paul, this is a very curious case, isn't it?
TEMPLE:	What do you mean?
STEVE:	Well, take Red Harris. Red was mixed up in this case, he must have been otherwise he never would have been murdered. But Red Harris was hardly the sort of man to associate with young Ferguson.
TEMPLE:	It rather depends what young Ferguson was up to.
STEVE:	And then take this man tonight – who impersonated Wyman – he was a very different type from Red Harris.
TEMPLE:	Give me the Red Harris type every time!
STEVE:	Yes, I know darling, but what I'm getting at is this. It seems to me that we're up against something a little different this time. We're up against something …

There is a knock at the door.

STEVE:	There's someone at the door.
TEMPLE:	All right, I'll go.

A pause.

The knock is repeated.

The door is opened.

CHARLES:	Mr Temple? (*RUDOLF CHARLES is in his late twenties. He has a pleasant Central European accent*)

TEMPLE: Yes?

CHARLES: My name is Rudolf Charles. I'm a friend of
             Max Wyman's. I spoke to Sir Graham Forbes
             on the telephone this afternoon and he said …

TEMPLE: Oh yes! Come in, Mr Charles! Delighted to
             meet you!

The door closes.

CHARLES: I hope I'm not intruding.

TEMPLE: Not at all. As a matter of fact I intended to call
             on you later this evening. Oh, may I introduce
             my wife?

CHARLES: How do you do, Mrs Temple?

TEMPLE: This is Rudolf Charles, Steve. The young man
             Sir Graham mentioned. He's a friend of Max
             Wyman's – the real Max Wyman.

STEVE: How do you do, Mr Charles?

CHARLES: (*Puzzled*) What do you mean, Mr Temple – the
             real Max Wyman?

TEMPLE: A short while ago a young man called on us
             and introduced himself as Max Wyman …

CHARLES: Max is in Scotland – he's not due back until
             tomorrow night. I told Sir Graham that on the
             telephone when he …

TEMPLE: Yes, I know you did.

CHARLES: But why should anyone want to impersonate
             Max?

TEMPLE: Mr Charles, tell me – did you tell anyone that
             you'd spoken to Sir Graham?

CHARLES: No.

TEMPLE: You didn't mention to anyone – to any of your
             friends for instance – that I was staying here
             and that Sir Graham wanted Max Wyman to
             look me up.

CHARLES: No. Why should I? (*Amused*) Mr Temple, it's common knowledge that you are staying here – in Oxford, I mean. Haven't you seen the evening papers?

TEMPLE: Yes, but it isn't common knowledge that Sir Graham tried to telephone Wyman.

CHARLES: No. I see your point. I'm the only person who knew about the telephone call.

TEMPLE: Exactly.

CHARLES: Well, I can assure you I didn't mention it to anyone. (*A shrug*) It didn't seem very important. (*Suddenly, pleasantly*) Mr Temple, I'll tell you why I called on you this evening. In one of the London papers there's a report that a man called Mackintosh …

TEMPLE: Reggie Mackintosh?

CHARLES: That's right. There's a report that he saw Richard Ferguson in London two days ago. He seems quite adamant about it. He swears it was Ferguson he saw.

TEMPLE: Well?

CHARLES: Well – is there any truth in it?

TEMPLE: Supposing I said that there was some truth in it?

CHARLES: (*Smiling*) Then that would explain a great deal.

TEMPLE: What do you mean?

CHARLES: The morning after Richard Ferguson was murdered – or, shall we say, the morning after the body was discovered? – a friend of mine, called Maureen Sharpe, thought she saw Richard go into The Encounter. She actually followed him into the restaurant. When she got inside however the place was empty. Naturally

	Elliot laughed at her – he told her it was an hallucination.
TEMPLE:	Elliot?
CHARLES:	Yes, Mark Elliot – he owns The Encounter.
STEVE:	Was Mr Elliot a friend of Richard's?
CHARLES:	Yes, in a casual way.
TEMPLE:	I see.
CHARLES:	(*Seriously*) Mr Temple, do you think my friend – Maureen – really did see Richard?
TEMPLE:	(*Ignoring CHARLES's question*) How well did you know Richard Ferguson?
CHARLES:	Oh, not very well. We met at debating societies and that sort of thing. He wasn't a personal friend of mine.
TEMPLE:	Was he a personal friend of Miss Sharpe's?
CHARLES:	No, I don't think she'd met him more than two or three times.
TEMPLE:	(*Deliberately casually*) Then she was probably mistaken – it was most likely someone else she saw. (*Pleasantly*) We're just going down to have a drink, Charles – will you join us?
CHARLES:	I should like to but I have a date at half past seven. Some other time perhaps?
TEMPLE:	Yes, of course.
CHARLES:	Goodbye, Mrs Temple.
STEVE:	Goodnight, Mr Charles.
CHARLES:	I'll get Max to give you a ring the moment he returns from Scotland.
TEMPLE:	Thank you.

The door opens.

| TEMPLE: | (*A sudden thought*) Oh, by the way – did you ever meet a friend of young Ferguson's called Jonathan? |
| CHARLES: | Jonathan? |

67

TEMPLE: Yes.
CHARLES: No, I'm afraid not. Why?
TEMPLE: I wondered, that's all. Goodnight, Mr Charles.
CHARLES: Goodnight.

The door closes.

STEVE: Well, I don't care for that young man!
TEMPLE: You don't? Why not?
STEVE: He's far too attractive! And that accent! (*Imitating Charles's accent*) I'll get Max to ring you the moment he returns from Scotland.
TEMPLE: (*Laughing*) Come on, let's go down and have a drink.
STEVE: (*Seriously*) Paul … Why do you think Reggie Mackintosh gave that story to the press – about seeing Richard, I mean? Sir Graham told him to keep it quiet – he made quite a point of it.
TEMPLE: (*Thoughtfully*) Yes, he did, didn't he, Steve? Come along, darling – drinks.

FADE SCENE.

FADE UP background conversation noises of the main hall of the hotel.

TEMPLE: I'll see you in the lounge, Steve. I'm going to get some cigarettes.
STEVE: All right, dear.

A pause.

TEMPLE: Have you any cigarettes?
PORTER: I'm sorry, sir. I haven't got any here at the moment.
TEMPLE: All right. I'll get some at the bar.
PORTER: Very good, sir. Oh, good evening, Mrs Russell!
MAVIS: (*A pleasant, attractive voice: she is in her early forties*) Good evening, George! And how are you these days?

68

PORTER: Oh, I'm very well thank you. Can't grumble at all. It's a long time since we saw you, madam.

MAVIS: Yes. George, tell me – have you got a Mr Temple staying in the hotel?

PORTER: (*Surprised*) You mean Paul Temple?

MAVIS: Yes.

PORTER: (*Laughing*) Why, this is Mr Temple, madam!

MAVIS: (*Taken aback*) Oh! Oh, I beg your pardon!

TEMPLE: Mrs Russell?

MAVIS: Yes …

TEMPLE: What can I do for you?

MAVIS: Well, I don't know whether you've heard of me or not, Mr Temple, but I was a friend of Richard Ferguson's and …

TEMPLE: Yes, of course I've heard of you, Mrs Russell! As a matter of fact my wife's just finished reading a book of yours – The Purple Moon.

MAVIS: Oh – that!

TEMPLE laughs.

MAVIS: Curiously enough, Mr Temple, I've just finished a book of yours – The Dorking Murder.

TEMPLE: Oh – that!

TEMPLE and MAVIS both laugh.

MAVIS: The papers say that you're investigating the Ferguson case, Mr Temple – is that true?

TEMPLE: I'm certainly very interested in the case.

MAVIS: Well, perhaps you don't know, but I'm considered a suspect in the Ferguson case.

TEMPLE: Really?

MAVIS: Oh, yes! I'm the notorious Mrs Russell. The seductive siren who influenced an impressionable young undergraduate.

TEMPLE: You sound as if you've been talking to Dinah
            Nelson.
MAVIS: Oh, she isn't the only one who thinks that way.
            Half Oxford is convinced that if I didn't
            actually murder Richard I most certainly had
            something to do with it.
TEMPLE: Have you seen tonight's paper, Mrs Russell?
MAVIS: Of course I have. That's why I'm here. I
            wouldn't have known that you were in Oxford
            if I hadn't read … Oh, you mean that absurd
            story! Of course Richard's dead. I helped to
            identify his body. I think this man –
            Mackintosh – must be out of his mind! I'm
            surprised at the press falling for such nonsense!
TEMPLE: You don't think that Reggie Mackintosh did
            see Richard Ferguson?
MAVIS: Of course he didn't!
TEMPLE: Supposing I told you that at least two other
            people had seen him?
MAVIS: Then I should say that Mr Mackintosh wasn't
            the only person who needed his head
            examined!
TEMPLE: (*Laughing*) Let's join my wife, Mrs Russell.
            She's in the lounge.
MAVIS: But – you don't really believe this story, do
            you? You don't think that Richard Ferguson is
            alive?
TEMPLE: (*A moment*) Yes, I do.
MAVIS: But it's nonsense! Absolute nonsense!
            (*Casually: so completely convinced*) In any
            case, I know he's dead.
TEMPLE: How do you know?
MAVIS: I had a letter this afternoon – from the man who
            murdered him.

70

Dramatic FADE UP of music.

FADE DOWN of music.
FADE UP of STEVE speaking.

STEVE: Do sit down, Mrs Russell.

MAVIS: Thank you.

STEVE: Paul, you have the other chair – I'll sit on the bed.

TEMPLE: Sorry dragging you up to our bedroom but we can at least talk more freely here.

MAVIS: Yes of course.

TEMPLE: Now, Mrs Russell – about that letter.

MAVIS: Before I show you the letter I want to talk to you about Richard. I want to make quite certain that you understand my side of the story.

TEMPLE: I'll do my best.

MAVIS: I wasn't in love with Richard Ferguson and I never made love to him either. Richard was a boy with talent, but like most young writers he needed encouragement. Not just the encouragement of friends but the encouragement and advice of another writer – a professional writer.

STEVE: Like yourself for instance?

MAVIS: Exactly, Mrs Temple. I read pretty well everything Richard wrote. I criticised his work, I lent him books, I introduced him to influential people. If that's considered to be exercising an evil influence then I certainly exercised it over Richard Ferguson.

TEMPLE: Go on, Mrs Russell.

MAVIS: When Richard was murdered certain people suggested I was responsible. Oh, they didn't actually accuse me of committing the murder,

71

	but – they insinuated that I'd introduced him to the wrong people.
TEMPLE:	Insinuations are of very little importance; it's what the police think that really matters.
MAVIS:	Yes, but that's just the point. I believe the police think that I really did have something to do with the murder.
TEMPLE:	Show me the letter you received.
MAVIS:	It's simply a typewritten note – unsigned. It arrived by the first post this morning.
TEMPLE:	Let me see it …

A pause.

STEVE:	Read it out, Paul.
TEMPLE:	(*Reading*) "Dear Mrs Russell, I feel quite sure that you, more than anyone else, would like to have the enclosed. It belonged to Richard Ferguson" … What makes you think this note was sent by the person that murdered Ferguson?
MAVIS:	Because this is what he sent me!
STEVE:	The signet ring!
MAVIS:	Yes! If the person who wrote that note didn't murder Richard then how did they get hold of the signet ring?
TEMPLE:	Is it Ferguson's ring?
MAVIS:	Yes.
TEMPLE:	You're sure?
MAVIS:	Quite sure.
TEMPLE:	So you believe that young Ferguson was murdered and the murderer stole the signet ring and then, for some reason which isn't at all clear, sent it to you?
MAVIS:	Yes.
TEMPLE:	You really think that's what happened?

MAVIS:	Yes, I do.
TEMPLE:	(*A moment*) I see.
STEVE:	Where was the letter posted, Paul?
TEMPLE:	London, S.W.7. last night. Did you ever meet a friend of Richard Ferguson's called Jonathan?
MAVIS:	Jonathan who?
TEMPLE:	I don't know. The reason I ask is because a postcard arrived after the murder – it was signed Jonathan. So far the police have been unable to locate the sender.
MAVIS:	Is it important?
TEMPLE:	Everything is important when you are investigating a murder.
STEVE:	Mrs Russell, have you met Richard's parents?
MAVIS:	No.
STEVE:	We travelled back from New York with them. That's how my husband became interested in the case.
MAVIS:	I see.
TEMPLE:	Have you looked at this ring very closely?
MAVIS:	Why?
TEMPLE:	Have you noticed what's on the inside?
MAVIS:	No …
TEMPLE:	There are some letters and numbers – you can see them quite clearly. Look …
MAVIS:	(*Looking at the ring*) A4 … D4 … That's funny. I never noticed that before.
TEMPLE:	You've no idea what it means?
MAVIS:	Not the slightest.
STEVE:	Paul, if you take a ring to be enlarged don't they sometime scrawl numbers on the inside?
MAVIS:	Yes, I think they do.
TEMPLE:	(*Examining the ring*) I don't think this ring has been enlarged, at least it doesn't look like it.

	(*Suddenly*) I'm afraid I shall have to keep it – and the note – for the time being.
MAVIS:	Yes, of course.
TEMPLE:	Mrs Russell, you said you introduced Richard to quite a lot of people – influential people.
MAVIS:	Yes.
TEMPLE:	Did you introduce him to a man called Mark Elliot?
MAVIS:	(*Surprised*) Yes, I did. Why do you ask?
TEMPLE:	I wondered, that's all.
MAVIS:	Do you know Mark?
TEMPLE:	No.
MAVIS:	He's a very charming man, and very influential.
TEMPLE:	He runs a restaurant, doesn't he?
MAVIS:	(*Laughing*) He owns a restaurant – The Encounter. He also owns six bookshops, a department store, three real estate companies and a couple of provincial newspapers.
TEMPLE:	He certainly does sound influential!
STEVE:	We always seem to be bumping into sleek, suave young men who own nightclubs, don't we, darling?
MAVIS:	(*Faintly irritated by STEVE's remark*) Elliot isn't suave, Mrs Temple, and he isn't sleek either, and if it comes to that he doesn't own a nightclub. The Encounter is a restaurant and a very good restaurant too. If you're staying in Oxford for any length of time you'd be well advised to try it.
TEMPLE:	How old is Mr Elliot?
MAVIS:	About forty-six or seven. He was intended for the diplomatic service but he suddenly developed an absolute passion for business. I don't know anyone who really enjoys business

74

	– I mean ordinary, dull, down to earth business – quite so much as Mark.
STEVE:	Is he married?
MAVIS:	No, he's a bachelor, Mrs Temple, and a teetotaller. (*Laughing*) He goes to bed with a glass of milk and a balance sheet. Still, I'm very fond of him.
STEVE:	Does he live in Oxford?
MAVIS:	Yes – he has a very beautiful flat above the restaurant.
TEMPLE:	Was he a great friend of Richard Ferguson's?
MAVIS:	No, I don't really think Mark liked Richard very much. You know, Richard was a very peculiar boy. I was very fond of him, but – well – he could be very difficult at times.
STEVE:	How do you mean – difficult?
MAVIS:	Well, sometimes he talked too loudly and too often about things he knew very little about. I understand him. I knew he was eager and young and that it was all part of a boyish enthusiasm. I'm afraid Mark wasn't quite so tolerant.
TEMPLE:	I can understand that. (*Suddenly*) Mrs Russell, don't you sometimes write for a magazine called The New Feature?
MAVIS:	Yes – I write a weekly article for them under the name of Europa. Why?
TEMPLE:	Someone sent Mr and Mrs Ferguson a copy of the magazine. The name Europa was underlined. The person who underlined it also scribbled the words – "If you want to know who murdered your son – ask Europa"!
MAVIS:	(*Angrily*) What a beastly thing to do!

TEMPLE: I'm inclined to agree. Have you any idea who did it?

MAVIS: No. No, I haven't – it might have been one of so many of my ... dear ... friends. Mr Temple, tell me, quite frankly – do you think I murdered Richard Ferguson?

TEMPLE: No, I don't – for the simple reason that I don't think he was murdered! But I'd still like to know who sent the Fergusons that magazine!

FADE UP of music.

FADE DOWN of music.

Slow FADE UP of background music of a small-piece restaurant orchestra: this is a small string orchestra playing modern but not 'hot' music.

There is a faint buzz of conversation which is typical of the main hall of an exclusive restaurant.

STEVE: Mrs Russell was right about this restaurant, Paul. It certainly is attractive!

TEMPLE: Yes. I think perhaps they could have done with just one chandelier less.

STEVE: Mm – perhaps.

WAITER: Good evening, sir. Have you reserved a table, sir?

TEMPLE: No. I'm afraid we haven't.

WAITER: I shall have to keep you waiting about a quarter of an hour, sir. I'm sorry.

TEMPLE: That's all right.

STEVE: Where is the Ladies cloakroom?

WAITER: On the first floor, madam.

STEVE: Thank you. See you later, darling.

TEMPLE: Yes, all right, Steve. (*To the WAITER*) You seem very busy tonight.

WAITER:	We're like this most nights, sir. On Saturdays it's quite impossible to get a table unless you reserve well in advance.
TEMPLE:	How long have you been open?
WAITER:	Just about a year, sir.
TEMPLE:	Well, it's obviously a great success.
WAITER:	Yes, it is, sir. Can I get you anything to drink?
TEMPLE:	No thanks. I think I'll wait for my wife.
WAITER:	Very good, sir.
DINAH:	(*Brightly, rather pleased with life*) Why, hello, Mr Temple!
TEMPLE:	Hello, Miss Nelson!
DINAH:	Was that Mrs Temple just going upstairs?
TEMPLE:	Yes.
DINAH:	Do you know, I thought it was! I said to Reggie that … Oh, I beg your pardon! This is my brother-in-law – Reggie Mackintosh.
TEMPLE:	(*Significantly*) Yes, we've met before, haven't we, Mr Mackintosh?
REGGIE:	Yes, we have …
TEMPLE:	The last time we met you promised …
REGGIE:	I know! I know exactly what you're going to say! Mr Temple's annoyed with me, Dinah – an' for a very good reason too, I'm afraid.
DINAH:	What do you mean, Reggie?
REGGIE:	Well – go on, you'd better tell her, Mr Temple.
TEMPLE:	Sir Graham Forbes – in other words Scotland Yard – told your brother-in-law that under no circumstances must he tell the press that he'd seen Richard Ferguson.
REGGIE:	Well, I did tell them! I'm sorry but – the fact is I had a few drinks with a pal o' mine – one of the Fleet Street boys. He started to talk about the Ferguson case an' – well, I just couldn't

	contain myself. I simply had to tell him that I'd seen Richard.
DINAH:	But, Mr Temple, what does it matter what the newspapers say? The fact remains that Richard's alive and I'm sure there's a perfectly simple explanation to the whole mystery.
TEMPLE:	I hope you're right, but don't forget if the murdered man wasn't Richard Ferguson he was certainly "somebody" and someone murdered him.
DINAH:	You're not suggesting that Richard did!
TEMPLE:	Well, that's the only simple explanation I can think of, Miss Nelson.
REGGIE:	You mean Richard invited this man to his flat, shot him in the head so that the body couldn't be recognised, dressed him up in his own clothes and then …
DINAH:	(*Angrily*) That's absurd!
TEMPLE:	Why? Someone committed the murder.
DINAH:	Yes, well I'm quite sure that Richard didn't!
TEMPLE:	How long are you staying in Oxford, Mr Mackintosh?
REGGIE:	Oh, a day or so. I usually pop up to Oxford two or three times a week. I'm in the textile business. Waingoing and Taplow, the wholesalers – you've probably heard of them.
TEMPLE:	Yes, I have.
REGGIE:	They're a tough firm to work for but it you get results they don't complain.
DINAH:	(*Rather subdued*) I think we ought to be making a move, Reggie. I don't want to be late.
REGGIE:	Yes, all right, Dinah.
TEMPLE:	Oh, Miss Nelson …
DINAH:	Yes?

TEMPLE:	(*Taking the ring from his pocket*) Have you seen this before?
DINAH:	(*Tensely*) Where did you get that ring from?
TEMPLE:	You haven't answered my question.
DINAH:	(*Very tensely*) Where did you get that ring from?
TEMPLE:	Is it Richard Ferguson's?
DINAH:	Yes …
TEMPLE:	You're sure?
DINAH:	Of course I'm sure! Please let me have it!
REGGIE:	(*Pacifying DINAH*) Now, Dinah … Dinah, don't be stupid, my dear!
TEMPLE:	Why do you want the ring, Miss Nelson?
DINAH:	Because I haven't got anything of Richard's … I haven't got anything to remember him by, and I would like just one …
TEMPLE:	Nothing to remember him by? Now you're talking as if Richard was dead and only a moment ago you seemed quite convinced that he wasn't.
DINAH:	Mr Temple, please, please – please let me have that ring.
TEMPLE:	I'm sorry, Miss Nelson …
DINAH:	What are you going to do with it?
TEMPLE:	There is only one thing I can do – hand it over to the police.
DINAH:	But, Mr Temple, don't you realise …
REGGIE:	Now don't be stupid! If Mr Temple considers that the ring is important it's his duty to hand it over to the police. After all, Dinah, don't forget Mr Temple is a private investigator. So far as the police are concerned, he's in the same position as you or I.

DINAH:	I'm sorry, Mr Temple, I didn't mean to be stupid.
REGGIE:	Come along, Dinah!
MARK:	(*A pleasant, cultured – if faintly suave – man in his late forties*) Good evening, Dinah! Good evening, Mackintosh!
REGGIE:	(*Pleasantly, always rather impressed by MARK ELLIOT*) Oh, good evening, sir.
MARK:	Are you just leaving?
REGGIE:	Yes – we've had an excellent dinner and I'm just taking Dinah home.
MARK:	You look rather tired, Dinah.
DINAH:	Yes, I've had rather a busy time just lately …
REGGIE:	Oh, I beg your pardon! May I introduce Mr Temple? Paul Temple – Mark Elliot.
MARK:	Oh – how do you do, Mr Temple. This is a pleasant surprise. I heard that you were in Oxford.
TEMPLE:	Yes, most people seem to have heard.
DINAH:	Goodnight, Mr Temple.
TEMPLE:	Goodnight, Miss Nelson.
DINAH:	Goodnight, Mark.
MARK:	Goodnight, Dinah.
REGGIE:	If you should want to get in touch with me, Mr Temple, I'm staying at The Cromwell – I shall be there until Friday.
TEMPLE:	I'll remember that. Goodnight!
REGGIE:	Goodnight.
A pause.	
MARK:	Are you alone?
TEMPLE:	No, as a matter of fact I'm waiting for my wife.
MARK:	May I offer you a drink while you're waiting?
TEMPLE:	Well – thank you.
MARK:	Let's go into the cocktail bar.

FADE SCENE.

FADE UP background conversation of a small, intimate cocktail bar.

BOBBY: Good evening, Mr Elliot.

MARK: Good evening, Bobby. What would you like, Temple?

TEMPLE: May I have a dry martini?

MARK: Yes, of course. A dry martini, Bobby – and the usual for me.

BOBBY: Yes, sir.

MARK: I suppose you've seen the story – in the papers – about Richard Ferguson?

TEMPLE: Yes.

MARK: Is it true?

TEMPLE: Yes – I think it is.

MARK: In other words young Ferguson's alive?

TEMPLE: Yes.

MARK: Well, I'm delighted to hear it.

TEMPLE: Why? Was Ferguson a friend of yours?

MARK: No; to be candid I couldn't tolerate the fellow. I prefer my intellectuals to be over forty. No, the reason I'm delighted to hear that he's alive is simply because, well …

TEMPLE: Go on …

MARK: I find this rather difficult to put into words.

TEMPLE: You can speak quite freely to me.

MARK: I'm sure I can; it isn't that, but – (*Frankly*) Well, look, Temple. The morning I heard that Richard Ferguson was murdered I was terrified – absolutely terrified. You see, I had a motive for murdering young Ferguson – a very strong motive.

TEMPLE: What was your motive?

81

MARK:	(*Smiling*) Didn't Mavis Russell tell you?
TEMPLE:	(*A moment*) How did you know that I'd seen Mrs Russell?
MARK:	(*Quite pleasantly*) It's quite a small place Oxford, you know – it's surprising how quickly things like that get round.
TEMPLE:	(*A moment*) You still haven't answered my question. What was your motive?
MARK:	Richard Ferguson was blackmailing me.

Dramatic FADE UP of music.

Slow FADE DOWN of music.
A door opens.
FADE UP STEVE.

STEVE:	(*Yawning*) Gosh, I'm tired!
TEMPLE:	Did you like that restaurant?
STEVE:	Yes, I did, darling. It's a little flamboyant perhaps, but – I liked it.
TEMPLE:	And what about Mark Elliot?
STEVE:	I don't quite know what to make of him. He's a peculiar mixture, isn't he?
TEMPLE:	He certainly is. Do you know what he told me, Steve – before you joined us?
STEVE:	No?
TEMPLE:	He told me that Richard Ferguson has been blackmailing him.
STEVE:	What!
TEMPLE:	He told me, in confidence, that during the past six weeks young Ferguson had had about two thousand pounds out of him.
STEVE:	Did he tell you what young Ferguson was blackmailing him about?
TEMPLE:	No, he didn't.

STEVE: But Richard must have had plenty of money: his father's very well off.

TEMPLE: That doesn't mean to say that Richard was. Steve, what did you think of Mrs Russell?

STEVE: Well – much to my surprise, darling, I took rather a favourable view of her.

TEMPLE: (*Laughing*) Yes. Mavis Russell is a very smart woman.

STEVE: (*Yawning*) What do you mean by that?

TEMPLE: She can adapt herself to the company she's with. I say, by Timothy, you are tired, aren't you?

STEVE: (*Still yawning*) Exhausted. What time is it?

TEMPLE: Quarter to twelve.

STEVE: Oh, I thought it was much later than that. (*Struggling with her dress*) This is a frightful dress to get off.

TEMPLE: Here, let me unzip you …

STEVE: (*A moment, buried in the dress*) You know, Paul, I think that …

TEMPLE: Don't talk, pull!

STEVE: (*The dress is off, relieved*) Oh, that's better!

TEMPLE: Now – what were you going to say?

STEVE: Give me my dressing gown. I was going to say, it's my opinion that Mavis Russell deliberately fosters the impression that …

The telephone rings.

A pause.

STEVE: Who do you think that is?

TEMPLE: It might be Sir Graham.

STEVE: It's rather late for Sir Graham, surely …

TEMPLE: (*On the phone*) Hello?

| PORTER: | (*On the other end of the phone, an internal line*) There's a call for you, sir. Hold on a moment, please. |

A pause.

| STEVE: | Who is it? |
| TEMPLE: | I don't know. |

A moment.

PORTER:	You're through!
TEMPLE:	Hello?
RICHARD:	(*On the other end: an educated voice, at the moment he is tense and emotional*) Paul Temple?
TEMPLE:	Yes?
RICHARD:	This is <u>Richard</u> Ferguson speaking.
TEMPLE:	What?
RICHARD:	Mr Temple, please, listen. This is urgent. I haven't a lot of time.
TEMPLE:	All right – go on.
RICHARD:	I understand you've got the signet ring – the one that Mavis Russell gave you?
TEMPLE:	Yes.
RICHARD:	Well, I want you to take it to Mrs Gulliver – take it to her first thing tomorrow morning.
TEMPLE:	Mrs Gulliver?
RICHARD:	Yes, she's my landlady. Mrs Gulliver – 3 Mortimer Close. Have you got the address?
TEMPLE:	Yes. 3, Mortimer Close.
RICHARD:	(*Tensely*) Now listen, Temple – if you do what I tell you and take the ring to Mrs Gulliver – I give you my word of honour that I'll meet you tomorrow night – anywhere – anytime – and tell you – exactly … what … this … is … all … about …

TEMPLE:	How will you know whether Mrs Gulliver has got the ring or not?
RICHARD:	Don't worry – I'll know.
TEMPLE:	All right. I'll do what you say.
RICHARD:	Good! Now where do you want me to meet you?
TEMPLE:	You suggest the place – I'll be there.
RICHARD:	Do you know The Encounter – the restaurant?
TEMPLE:	(*Surprised*) Yes …
RICHARD:	If Mrs Gulliver gets the ring I'll see you there tomorrow night – ten o'clock. O.K.?
TEMPLE:	I can depend on that?
RICHARD:	You can depend on it, Temple!
TEMPLE:	Good! I'll be there.
RICHARD:	Right! … Goodbye!

TEMPLE replaces his receiver.

STEVE:	(*Excited*) Paul, what is it?
TEMPLE:	(*Excited*) It was young Ferguson!
STEVE:	What?!
TEMPLE:	(*Feeling in his pockets, tensely*) Steve, where did I put that ring?
STEVE:	You put it in your pocket – at least, you said you did.
TEMPLE:	(*Searching in his pockets*) Yes, I put it in my inside pocket – the ticket pocket. I'm sure I did. I'm absolutely positive I did! (*Still searching*) Steve, it's gone!
STEVE:	Darling, it can't. Now, just think … when did you see it last?
TEMPLE:	I showed it to Dinah Nelson, it was while you were in the cloakroom. (*Slowly*) Then I put it back in my inside pocket and deliberately … (*He stops*)
STEVE:	What is it?

85

TEMPLE: I was just thinking … Reggie Mackintosh stood very close to me … while Dinah Nelson was saying goodnight to Elliot.

STEVE: I don't think it was Reggie Mackintosh, Paul.

TEMPLE: Why do you say that?

STEVE: I think Elliot took it! I think he took it just as I walked into the cocktail bar.

TEMPLE: But what makes you think …

STEVE: Don't you remember? You both stood up. You were standing very close together. Elliot took you by the arm, moved the table slightly so that I could get by, and then …

TEMPLE: Yes! You're right, Steve!

There is a knock on the door.

TEMPLE: Come in!

The door opens.

STEVE: Why, Mrs Ferguson!

HELEN: Good evening, Mrs Temple!

TEMPLE: Come in, Mrs Ferguson!

HELEN: I'm so sorry to disturb you, but we did call round earlier this evening.

TEMPLE: We've been out all evening – we've only been back five or ten minutes.

STEVE: Are you staying here, Mrs Ferguson?

HELEN: Yes, we're just along the corridor. We arrived about eight o'clock. We came down to see Mrs Gulliver, that's Richard's landlady, Mr Temple …

TEMPLE: Yes, I know. Go on Mrs Ferguson …

HELEN: Well, she telephoned us this morning. The poor dear seemed rather worried …

TEMPLE: What about exactly?

HELEN: Well, apparently a letter arrived for Richard this morning and Mrs Gulliver opened it by mistake.

TEMPLE: What sort of letter?

HELEN: Well, that's just the point. The letter doesn't seem important – it doesn't seem at all important – and yet …

TEMPLE: Well?

HELEN: It's from that friend of Richard's – the one no one seems to know anything about … Jonathan!

FADE UP of music.

END OF EPISODE THREE

EPISODE FOUR

THE ENCOUNTER

OPEN TO:

HELEN: ... We arrived about eight o'clock. We came
              down to see Mrs Gulliver, that's Richard's
              landlady, Mr Temple ...
TEMPLE: Yes, I know. Go on Mrs Ferguson ...
HELEN: Well, she telephoned us this morning. The poor
              dear seemed rather worried ...
TEMPLE: What about exactly?
HELEN: Well, apparently a letter arrived for Richard
              this morning and Mrs Gulliver opened it by
              mistake.
TEMPLE: What sort of letter?
HELEN: Well, that's just the point. The letter doesn't
              seem important – it doesn't seem at all
              important – and yet ...
TEMPLE: Well?
HELEN: It's from that friend of Richard's – the one no
              one seems to know anything about ...
              Jonathan!
STEVE: Jonathan!
HELEN: Yes ...
TEMPLE: May I see it ...
There is a knock on the door.
HELEN: I expect that's Robert.
The door opens.
STEVE: Come in, Mr Ferguson.
ROBERT: Thank you, Mrs Temple. I had a hunch that
              you'd be here, Helen.
HELEN: (*Tensely*) I wanted Mr Temple to see the letter,
              Robert. Mrs Gulliver seemed to think it was
              important.
ROBERT: Now how can it be important? It's just a letter
              wishing a guy a happy birthday!

STEVE: What does it say, Paul?

TEMPLE: (*Reading*) "Dear Richard, … This is just to wish you a happy birthday. Hope to see you at the end of the week. Regards, Jonathan."

ROBERT: Well, does that strike you as being a very mysterious letter?

TEMPLE: You say Mrs Gulliver opened it by mistake?

ROBERT: That's right. She was in quite a slap about it.

TEMPLE: When did you see her?

ROBERT: This evening. Helen suddenly got it into her head that Richard might try and contact Mrs Gulliver. She's made the old girl promise that if he does she'll get in touch with us straight away.

TEMPLE: (*Thoughtfully*) I see.

ROBERT: Look, it seems to me there's a perfectly simple explanation for all this Jonathan business.

TEMPLE: What is the simple explanation?

ROBERT: Jonathan is a friend of Richard's: he's on holiday and he hasn't taken the trouble to read the newspapers. I know I don't on holiday. He simply doesn't know anything about the murder and Richard's disappearance.

TEMPLE: No, I don't think it's quite as simple as that; the police have been trying to find Jonathan but no one in Oxford seems to have heard of him.

ROBERT: What are you getting at?

STEVE: Well, if Jonathan was a friend of Richard's surely some of his other friends would at least have heard of him.

ROBERT: Yeah – you'd certainly think so.

TEMPLE: Ferguson, tell me: was that the only reason you came to Oxford – to see Mrs Gulliver?

HELEN:	No, not entirely. I thought it might be a good idea if we met some of Richard's friends. You see, we hardly know anything about the sort of life he's been leading.
ROBERT:	My wife thinks he's being blackmailed; she's convinced that he didn't commit the murder himself and that someone is exercising a sort of influence over him.
TEMPLE:	Is that your opinion?
ROBERT:	(*Emphatically*) No, it isn't!
HELEN:	Robert!
ROBERT:	It's no good, Helen, I've got to speak my mind. Look, Temple, Richard's an only child. I don't want to get sentimental but he's the only thing we've got in the world. But, just because we're crazy about him it doesn't mean to say that we can't see straight. It doesn't mean to say that I can't see straight, anyway. Richard's always been a peculiar boy: he's selfish and egotistical …
HELEN:	No, Robert, he isn't!
ROBERT:	Listen, Helen, if Mr Temple's going to help us he's got to know the truth. I fly over to London pretty frequently, maybe five or six times a year. I always cable Richard when I leave New York. I'm still hoping that one day he'll take the trouble to meet me at the airport, or even at the hotel.
HELEN:	Now, Robert, just because he doesn't meet you at the airport …
ROBERT:	Did he send you a cable on your birthday, Helen?
HELEN:	No, but –

ROBERT:	Well, I sent him one – the day before telling him not to forget. He still forgot.
TEMPLE:	Did you make Richard an allowance?
ROBERT:	Why, sure! How do you think he lived?
TEMPLE:	Was it a generous one?
ROBERT:	It depends what you call generous.
TEMPLE:	Well –
ROBERT:	Six thousand dollars a year …
STEVE:	That's certainly generous!
TEMPLE:	Supposing he suddenly found that he needed money – quite a lot of money – two thousand pounds for instance, would he have asked you for it?
ROBERT:	Who else?
TEMPLE:	Would you have given it to him?
ROBERT:	Well, now, that depends. Two thousand pounds is a lot of money …
HELEN:	If Richard needed the money he'd have got it, Mr Temple – if not from his father then from me.
ROBERT:	But he didn't need money – he'd no financial troubles.
TEMPLE:	Are you sure?
ROBERT:	I'm positive.
TEMPLE:	M'm.
HELEN:	Mr Temple, you remember that magazine – the one that was sent to our hotel – with the message crawled across it?
TEMPLE:	Yes?
HELEN:	Well, we've discovered who Europa is. It's the nom-de-plume of a writer called Mavis Russell. Apparently she lives in Oxford and was a friend of Richard's.
ROBERT:	I expect Mr Temple already knows that.

TEMPLE: Yes, I do. I've met Mrs Russell.

HELEN: Was she a great friend of Richard's?

TEMPLE: Yes, I think she was.

STEVE: Mrs Russell still believes that it was Richard who was murdered.

HELEN: But that's absurd! I've seen Richard!

ROBERT: Richard's alive all right, there's no doubt about it. I only hope he stays that way.

HELEN: What do you mean, Robert?

ROBERT: I don't know whether Mr Temple agrees with me or not but I've got a hunch that it isn't only the police that Richard's trying to avoid.

HELEN: But who else would he want to avoid?

ROBERT: (*Puzzled*) I don't know. Maybe a woman – maybe Mrs Russell. (*With a shrug*) Or who knows? Maybe Jonathan.

FADE UP of music.

FADE DOWN of music.

FADE IN of TEMPLE.

TEMPLE: You're late!

STEVE: And you're making a beast of yourself!

TEMPLE: Well, this porridge is good. There's an excellent menu this morning, kippers, ham and eggs …

STEVE: Maybe, but just coffee for me!

TEMPLE: You know, you look like the morning after the night before!

STEVE: Thank you very much – it's taken me twenty minutes to look like this!

TEMPLE: (*Laughing*) I didn't mean that! I meant …

STEVE: Get on with your breakfast! Why the three cups?

TEMPLE: We've got company, darling!

STEVE:	Oh, lord! If there's anything I detest it's company for breakfast!
FORBES:	Do you, Steve? Sorry!
STEVE:	Sir Graham! I didn't mean you. When did you arrive?
FORBES:	About an hour ago.
TEMPLE:	Will you have some coffee?
FORBES:	Oh, thank you. Temple, I've just been on the phone to the Inspector – he confirms what I've told you.
STEVE:	What was that, Paul?
TEMPLE:	You remember the card – the first Jonathan card that arrived for Richard the morning after the murder?
STEVE:	Yes?
TEMPLE:	Well, the Yard have now discovered that the actual message on the card – the one supposed to be from Jonathan – was a blind …
FORBES:	Our cryptographical people got to work on it. Steve. They x-rayed it and discovered a secret message …
STEVE:	What do you mean – in invisible ink?
FORBES:	Yes. This was the real message – the one intended for Richard Ferguson.
STEVE:	Was it from Jonathan?
FORBES:	It was signed Jonathan, but – well – I suppose 'message' is hardly the right word, Temple.
TEMPLE:	It's just a list of letters and numbers, probably a cipher of some sort.
FORBES:	Show Steve the copy I gave you, Temple.
TEMPLE:	(*A moment*) Here you are, Steve. I don't suppose you'll make head or tail of it.
STEVE:	Thank you.

A tiny pause.

FORBES: We also examined the second card – the one
            that was intended for Dinah Nelson.

TEMPLE: The one that Reggie Mackintosh gave me?

FORBES: Yes. It was negative. Completely negative. It
            didn't reveal anything except the actual
            handwriting.

TEMPLE: Perhaps you'd better do the same to this letter.

FORBES: (*Takes the letter and starts to read*) "Dear
            Richard ... This is just to wish you ..."
            (*Looking up*) Where did you get this letter?

TEMPLE: Mrs Ferguson gave it to us last night.
            Apparently it arrived for Richard yesterday
            morning and his landlady, Mrs Gulliver,
            opened it by mistake. I think I'd better tell you
            what happened last night, Sir Graham. When
            we arrived here ...

STEVE: (*Looking up from the paper she is examining*)
            Just a moment, darling! (*Hesitantly*) This
            cipher, Sir Graham ...

FORBES: Yes?

STEVE: Look .... (*Reading*) "789267246ALEFLOELF"

TEMPLE: Well?

STEVE: If you split the numbers up and put the letters
            first. Say, take the first three numbers and the
            first three letters 789 ALE ...

TEMPLE: Yes ...

STEVE: Now take the next three numbers and the next
            three letters 267 FLO ...

FORBES: What are you getting at, Steve?

STEVE: They look like car registration numbers.

TEMPLE: (*Studying the paper*) 789 ALE ... 267 FLO ...
            246 ELF ... 246 ELF ...! By Timothy, she's
            right, Sir Graham! 246 ELF! I remember that
            number! That's the number of the car that Red

	Harris showed me – the Lombard – the one that was for sale!
FORBES:	Are you sure?
TEMPLE:	Absolutely positive!
STEVE:	(*Pleased with herself*) That good old intuition, eh?
FORBES:	I wonder if the others tie up in any way? I'll phone the numbers to Gerrard and get a check on them! Jolly good, Steve!
STEVE:	That'll cost you a new hat, darling.
TEMPLE:	Oh, yeah!
STEVE:	I've seen the very model. LSD 1414 …
TEMPLE:	What?
STEVE:	Fourteen guineas to you!

They all laugh.

FORBES:	You know, if this Jonathan business has got anything to do with the car racket, it's a curious coincidence.
TEMPLE:	What do you mean?
FORBES:	The French people picked up André Dumas last night. He's probably the biggest car racketeer on the continent.
TEMPLE:	Oh yes! I remember reading about him.
FORBES:	They've been after him for months. Now tell me what happened last night, Temple.
TEMPLE:	Well, just after I phoned you we ran into Mrs Russell: she gave me a signet ring – which she said was Richard's – and which she said had been sent to her through the post. Steve and I then went along to The Encounter – that's a restaurant owned by a man called Mark Elliot …
FORBES:	Yes, I've heard of it.

TEMPLE:	At The Encounter either Mark Elliot, Reggie Mackintosh or Dinah Nelson relieved me of the ring. When we got back to the hotel Richard Ferguson phoned me and …
FORBES:	Richard Ferguson!
TEMPLE:	Yes – and told me to take the ring to Mrs Gulliver. He said that if I did he would meet me tonight – at The Encounter – and explain what this is all about. After I'd spoken to Richard his mother turned up with the letter – the one I've given to you.
FORBES:	Did you tell her about the phone call?
TEMPLE:	No, I didn't mention the call or the ring.
FORBES:	M'm. It's a pity you lost that ring, Temple.
TEMPLE:	I agree, but I still intend to see Mrs Gulliver. If young Ferguson's in touch with Mrs Gulliver then it's ten to one that …
PORTER:	Excuse me, sir …
TEMPLE:	Yes?
PORTER:	There's a gentleman asking for you at the reception desk, Mr Temple, a Mr Charles, sir.
TEMPLE:	Oh, that's Rudolf Charles. Max Wyman's friend – the young fellow you spoke to on the telephone, Sir Graham.
FORBES:	Oh, yes.
TEMPLE:	Ask him to join us, will you?
PORTER:	Very good, sir.
FORBES:	(*After a moment*) You know, judging from what young Ferguson said it looks as if Mrs Gulliver's mixed up in this business.
TEMPLE:	Yes …
STEVE:	Have you met her, Sir Graham?
FORBES:	No, I haven't, Steve. But according to Inspector Gerrard she's rather a pleasant type of person.

STEVE: Was Richard Ferguson her only P.G.?

FORBES: Yes, but he wasn't exactly a P.G.; he rented the top of the house and turned it into a sort of flatlet: it was quite self-contained.

STEVE: I see. Paul, do you think that signet ring – or rather what was on the ring – ties up with the card that Jonathan sent?

TEMPLE: Yes, I think it does, Steve, but I can't quite see how.

FORBES: What was on the ring, Temple?

TEMPLE: A4 and D4 scratched. Apart from that it was just an ordinary signet ring.

STEVE: Here's Mr Charles. Good morning, Mr Charles.

CHARLES: Good morning.

TEMPLE: You know Sir Graham Forbes?

CHARLES: Oh, Sir Graham! How very fortunate! I almost telephoned you this morning, sir, but I thought perhaps I'd better have a word with Mr Temple first.

FORBES: Well, now you can have a word with both of us, Mr Charles.

CHARLES: (*Laughing*) Yes. (*Seriously*) Sir Graham, when I spoke to you on the phone I told you that Max Wyman was in Scotland and that he was due back in Oxford sometime tonight.

FORBES: Yes.

CHARLES: Well – it appears that I was mistaken. Max isn't in Scotland.

FORBES: He isn't?

CHARLES: I telephoned the Martins last night – they're the people he's supposed to be staying with. They haven't seen Max: he was expected on Tuesday but just didn't turn up.

FORBES: Where does he live?

CHARLES: His home's at Staveley just outside Windermere.

STEVE: He probably changed his mind and went home for two or three days.

CHARLES: No, his father – Lord Elsworth – telephoned me this morning. They haven't seen Max; they haven't even heard from him for almost a month.

TEMPLE: What's he like – Max Wyman?

FORBES: Oh, he's charming. You'd like him, Temple.

CHARLES: Everybody likes Max. I don't think there's a student in Oxford that Max doesn't know – I mean really know.

FORBES: Yes, that's why I wanted you to meet him.

TEMPLE: You misunderstood me, Sir Graham. I meant – what does he look like?

CHARLES: (*Thoughtfully*) He's about five feet eleven … dark …

FORBES: Clean shaven …

TEMPLE: How old is he?

FORBES: I should say he's about … twenty-two …

CHARLES: He's just twenty-three, Sir Graham.

FORBES: Oh …

A moment.

TEMPLE: How tall is Richard Ferguson?

CHARLES: (*Without seeing any significance in TEMPLE's remark*) Ferguson's about five feet eleven – perhaps six foot. As a matter of fact Ferguson always reminds me of Max. But Max has a much stronger personality. Oddly enough when you see them together there's a strange likeness … (*He stops: suddenly realising*) Mr Temple! Mr Temple, you don't think it was …?

FORBES: You don't think it was Max Wyman who was murdered?

TEMPLE: It's a possibility, Sir Graham, a strong possibility.

Dramatic FADE UP of music.

FADE DOWN of music.

FADE IN of TEMPLE.

TEMPLE: I'll give you a ring as soon as we've seen Mrs Gulliver, Sir Graham.

FORBES: Yes, all right, Temple. If you want to get in touch with me during the morning I shall be with Gerrard at police headquarters, Oxford 187.

TEMPLE: Right!

FORBES: I sincerely hope that you're wrong about Max Wyman.

TEMPLE: So do I, but I've got an uncanny feeling that I'm not.

PORTER: Your car's here, Mr Temple.

TEMPLE: Oh, thank you. Ready, Steve?

STEVE: Yes.

TEMPLE: See you later, Sir Graham.

FORBES: Yes. Goodbye, Steve.

STEVE: Goodbye.

FADE SCENE.

FADE UP a background of street noises.

FADE IN the ticking over of a stationary car.

TEMPLE opens the car door.

TEMPLE: I want you to take us to 3, Mortimer Close.

DRIVER: 3, Mortimer Close. Very good, sir.

STEVE: Wait a minute, Paul!

TEMPLE: What is it?

STEVE: Isn't that Mark Elliot? He's just driven up, darling – on the other side of the road.

TEMPLE: Yes! So it is!

We hear the sound of a horn blowing: MARK ELLIOT is blowing his horn in order to attract TEMPLE's attention.

STEVE: I think he wants to have a word with you.

TEMPLE: Yes. You get in the car, Steve. I'll join you in a minute.

STEVE: Yes, all right.

STEVE enters the car.

TEMPLE crosses the road to speak to MARK ELLIOT.

FADE UP the sound of MARK ELLIOT's car ticking over.

MARK: (*Pleasantly*) Hello! Where are you off to?

TEMPLE: Nowhere in particular. Where are you off to?

MARK: I'm going up to Town for two or three days.

TEMPLE: I see.

MARK: I'm very glad I spotted you, Temple. There's something I want to ask you.

TEMPLE: Well?

MARK: Did you lose anything last night – at the restaurant, I mean?

TEMPLE: Yes, as a matter of fact I did. I lost a ring.

MARK: A signet ring?

TEMPLE: Yes.

MARK: (*Smiling*) Is this it?

A pause.

TEMPLE: Yes …

MARK: One of the waiters said he thought it was yours. He found it in the cocktail bar. You must have dropped it.

TEMPLE: Yes, I must have done.

MARK: (*Closing the matter*) Well, I'm glad you've got it back anyway.

103

TEMPLE: But what made you think this ring belonged to me?
MARK: I've told you – one of the waiters said so.
TEMPLE: Yes, but it hasn't got my initials on it.
MARK: No, I noticed that. But Francois said he saw you with the ring. He said you showed it to Dinah Nelson.
TEMPLE: Yes, that's right. I did.
MARK: (*Smiling*) Well, there you are! Well, I'm delighted you've got it back anyway.
TEMPLE: Yes. Thanks very much. You must have a very observant staff at The Encounter.
MARK: (*Amused*) Oh, I don't know. We try to please. Goodbye.

FADE UP the sound of ELLIOT's car driving away.
FADE SCENE.

FADE IN of a car drawing to a standstill.
We hear the sound of a car door opening and closing.
DRIVER: This is Mortimer Close, sir. That's number 3 on the corner.
TEMPLE: Thank you.
DRIVER: Do you want me to wait?
TEMPLE: Yes, please. We shan't be very long.
DRIVER: O.K., sir! I'll turn the car round: it'll be over on the other side.
TEMPLE: Yes, all right. Come along, Steve!
FADE SCENE.

FADE UP of TEMPLE pulling the handle of an old-fashioned house bell: we can hear the bell ringing inside of the house.
The bell continues.
STEVE: Perhaps she's out, Paul.

TEMPLE: We'll wait a minute. (*A moment*) If she's out I'll dismiss the car and we'll go for a stroll and come back later.

STEVE: Yes. (*A pause*) I think there's someone coming!

The door is opened by EDDIE PAGET.

In the near background – actually in the hall of the house – a vacuum cleaner can be heard: it is standing stationary but is switched on.

EDDIE: (*About thirty: an obliging manner: very cockney*) Yes – what is it?

TEMPLE: Could we see Mrs Gulliver, please?

EDDIE: Is she expecting you?

TEMPLE: No, she isn't, but I think she'll see me. My name is Temple.

EDDIE: Temple?

TEMPLE: (*Faintly irritated*) Yes. Tell her I'm a friend of Richard Ferguson's.

EDDIE: Oh. Well – you'd better come in.

TEMPLE: Thank you.

TEMPLE and STEVE enter the house.

FADE UP the noise of the vacuum.

The door closes.

EDDIE: We're in a bit of a mess here. I'm just doing a spot of spring cleaning.

STEVE: Yes, I can see that.

TEMPLE: Do you work for Mrs Gulliver?

EDDIE: One day a week – that's all. Usually Tuesdays or Fridays. I'm with The Domestic Help Service. (*Curious*) I say, did you say you was a friend of Richard Ferguson's?

TEMPLE: Yes.

EDDIE: Well, what's 'appened to 'im? Is he dead or isn't he, that's what I'd like to know. The blinkin' papers just don't know what to make of it.

TEMPLE: I'm afraid we haven't a lot of time. If you don't mind we'd like to see Mrs Gulliver.

EDDIE: O.K. I'll give her a shout. She's upstairs. (*Shouting*) Mrs Gulliver! (*A moment: shouting*) Mrs Gulliver!

STEVE: Don't you think she'd hear you better if you switched the vacuum off?

EDDIE: She'd 'ear me all right, but it'd put paid to the vacuum. Took me 'alf an hour this morning to get the blinkin' thing started. (*Shouting*) Mrs Gulliver! (*A moment*) You'd better wait in the drawing room. I'll pop upstairs.

TEMPLE: Thank you.

A door opens.

EDDIE: I shan't be a jiffy.

TEMPLE and STEVE enter the drawing room.

The door closes.

FADE the noise of the vacuum cleaner to the background.

A slight pause.

STEVE: It's rather a nice room.

TEMPLE: Yes.

A moment.

STEVE: (*Thoughtfully*) Paul, I've been thinking about that ring that Elliot handed back to you. You're sure it's the same ring?

TEMPLE: Positive.

STEVE: Well, perhaps he was telling the truth. Perhaps you did drop it in the cocktail bar.

TEMPLE: (*Dubiously*) Um – perhaps.

In the background we hear the sound of the front door closing.

STEVE: Well, if you didn't drop it, I fail to see … Listen. (*Listening*) I thought I heard the front door closing.

TEMPLE: I'm rather doubtful about that young man …

STEVE: What do you mean?

TEMPLE: Why didn't he switch the vacuum off?

STEVE: He told you why.

The telephone commences to ring.

STEVE: He's spent half an hour trying to get it started.

The telephone continues to ring.

A pause.

The telephone continues.

STEVE: There doesn't seem to be anyone coming …

TEMPLE: No, I'll answer it.

TEMPLE lifts the receiver.

TEMPLE: (*On the phone*) Hello?

DINAH: (*On the other end of the line: tense*) Hello – is that 3, Mortimer Close?

TEMPLE: Yes, that's right.

DINAH: Is Mrs Gulliver there?

TEMPLE: She's upstairs at the moment.

DINAH: Well, could I speak to her, please? It's rather urgent.

TEMPLE: I'll see if I can get her … (*Suddenly*) Who is it speaking?

DINAH: This is Di … (*She suddenly changes her mind*)

DINAH replaces her receiver.

TEMPLE: (*Quickly*) Hello? Hello?!

STEVE: What's happened?

TEMPLE replaces the receiver.

TEMPLE: She's rung off!

STEVE: Who was it?

TEMPLE: It sounded to me like Dinah Nelson. I'm sure it was!

STEVE: What did she want?

TEMPLE: She asked for Mrs Gulliver – she said it was urgent. She sounded urgent too. Look here, I don't like the look of all this! It's about time Mrs Gulliver put in an appearance!

STEVE: Yes, I think so too.

TEMPLE: Come along, Steve!

The door opens.

FADE UP the sound of the vacuum which is still stationary but switched on.

TEMPLE: I don't see any sign of our cockney friend!

STEVE: No.

TEMPLE: I'll bet that was the front door we heard! I'm going to switch this thing off.

STEVE: Careful!

TEMPLE: It's all right!

TEMPLE switches off the vacuum.

TEMPLE: That's better!

STEVE: (*Suddenly*) Paul! Listen!

From upstairs we hear the voice of MRS GULLIVER. She is obviously in great pain: moaning.

TEMPLE: By Timothy!

STEVE: What is it?

TEMPLE: It must be Mrs Gulliver! That's why he kept the vacuum on, so that we shouldn't hear!

STEVE: Oh, Paul!

TEMPLE: She must be in here.

The door is thrown open.

FADE UP of MRS GULLIVER.

MRS GULLIVER: (*In great pain: almost unconscious*) Don't … Please don't … I haven't got the ring … I swear I haven't got it.

TEMPLE: Mrs Gulliver, listen!

MRS G: Please don't ... hurt ... me ... (*Her voice trails away*)

STEVE: (*Horrified*) Paul, she's in a dreadful state!

TEMPLE: (*Quickly*) Steve, go downstairs! Phone Sir Graham! Tell him what's happened and tell him we need an ambulance. Quickly, Steve! Quickly!

Dramatic FADE UP of music.

FADE DOWN of music.
FADE IN of SIR GRAHAM FORBES.

FORBES: ... Of course, on the other hand, you've got to bear in mind that if you'd arrived at the house a few minutes earlier ... (*He stops: interrupted by:*)

The opening of a door.

TEMPLE: Ah, here's the Inspector!

The door closes.

FORBES: Well, Gerrard?

GERRARD: (*Gloomily*) It doesn't look too good, sir.

FORBES: What does the doctor say?

GERRARD: He's still non-committal.

TEMPLE: Is she still unconscious?

GERRARD: Yes, and I'm afraid she will be for some time. I'm staying here – at the hospital, sir – just in case ...

FORBES: Yes, all right, Inspector. (*He looks at his watch*) Good Lord, is that the time? Well – I suppose I'd better be making a move. If you want me I shall be at the hotel.

GERRARD: Very good, sir.

FORBES: What do you intend to do, Temple?

TEMPLE: I'm going back to the hotel. I'm taking Steve to The Encounter later. You know, in spite of what's happened to Mrs Gulliver, I've got a feeling that Richard Ferguson might keep that appointment.

FORBES: I doubt it, Temple. I doubt it very much. Have you still got the ring?

TEMPLE: Yes. Do you want it, Sir Graham?

FORBES: No, you keep it for the time being. Did you examine it, Inspector?

GERRARD: Yes. We've made a detailed examination, sir.

FORBES: It looks to me like an ordinary signet ring – except for the markings.

GERRARD: Yes, it does to me, sir. Temple, that man who let you into Mrs Gulliver's … Would you recognise him again?

TEMPLE: Yes, I'm sure I would.

GERRARD: You'd never seen him before.

TEMPLE: No. I don't think so.

A knock is heard on the door.

GERRARD: Come in!

The door opens.

MESSEENGER: Excuse me, sir!

GERRARD: Come in, officer!

MESSENGER: Inspector Whiting asked me to deliver this message, sir.

GERRARD: Thank you.

GERRARD takes the envelope. He opens the letter.

A pause.

GERRARD: There's no reply.

MESSENGER: Thank you, sir.

The door closes.

FORBES: Well?

GERRARD: That letter Temple gave you, sir – the one he got from Mrs Ferguson.

FORBES: Yes?

110

GERRARD: The Yard have examined it – it's negative.

FORBES: That means the first Jonathan card had the cipher – the second card, that Mackintosh gave us, was negative and the letter's negative.

TEMPLE: (*Thoughtfully*) Yes …

GERRARD: There's something else on this report, sir.

FORBES: Well?

GERRARD: Temple was right. It was Max Wyman who was murdered!

FADE SCENE.

FADE IN of music: it is the orchestra at The Encounter.
FADE music to the background.

WAITER: Good evening, sir.

TEMPLE: Good evening.

WAITER: Have you reserved a table, sir?

TEMPLE: Yes, I have – the name's Temple.

WAITER: (*Perusing his list*) Oh, Mr Temple – a table for two. That's right.

TEMPLE: (*To the WAITER*) Has there been any message for me?

WAITER: I don't think so, sir. Wait a moment. (*A pause*) No, I'm afraid not, sir.

TEMPLE: Thank you. I'll be in the cocktail bar.

FADE music.
TEMPLE passes into the cocktail bar.
FADE UP a background of conversation.

BOBBY: Good evening, sir!

TEMPLE: Good evening! A dry martini, please.

BOBBY: Yes, sir.

MAVIS: Make that two, Bobby.

BOBBY: Very good, madam.

TEMPLE: Oh, hello, Mrs Russell!

MAVIS: Hello! Are you alone?

111

TEMPLE: Well, at the moment. I'm waiting for my wife.
MAVIS: Do … you … mind if I … join you?
MAVIS RUSELL is just a bit 'high'.
TEMPLE: No, of course not. I'm glad I bumped into you.
MAVIS: I'm glad I bumped into you too, Mr Temple.
              (*Very sorry for herself*) I'm very lonely …
TEMPLE: (*Non-comittally*) Oh …
MAVIS: I've been very lonely for a very long time.
TEMPLE: I'm sorry to hear that.
MAVIS: I'm sorry too. Still, I feel better now. Ever so
              much better. You're an oasis in my life – a
              mirage – the last train from Berlin …
BOBBY: (*Clearing his throat*) Two dry martinis.
TEMPLE: Thank you. Er – wouldn't you prefer an orange
              juice?
MAVIS: Me?
TEMPLE: Yes.
MAVIS: An … orange – juice?
TEMPLE: Yes.
MAVIS: (*With great charm*) Whatever gave you that
              idea?
TEMPLE: Well, I – er – thought perhaps it might make a
              change.
MAVIS: It would. A terrible change. A definite –
              deterioration …
TEMPLE: (*Quietly*) I don't know whether you know it or
              not, Mrs Russell, but you're just a little bit – er
              – high?
MAVIS: Who? Me?
TEMPLE: Yes.
MAVIS: A little bit – er – …?
TEMPLE: Yes.
MAVIS: Oh. Well, it's not surprising. I've had six
              scotch and martinis. No, that's not right, is it?

112

TEMPLE: I hope not.
MAVIS: Can't be right. Bobby, can you mix scotch and
             martini?
BOBBY: You can, madam – but I don't advise it.
MAVIS: Oh … well, cheers!
TEMPLE: Cheers.
A moment.
TEMPLE: I suppose you've heard about Mrs Gulliver?
MAVIS: No.
TEMPLE: She was brutally attacked.
MAVIS: Attacked?
TEMPLE: Yes, she's critically ill.
MAVIS: When – did – it – happen?
TEMPLE: This morning. Do you know why she was
             attacked?
MAVIS: No.
TEMPLE: They thought she had the signet ring.
MAVIS: Who's 'they'?
TEMPLE: Suppose you tell me, Mrs Russell.
MAVIS: I don't know. I don't know anything. I'm just a
             simple little girl who …
TEMPLE: (*Interrupting MAVIS*) You're not simple – and
             if it comes to that you're not little either.
             You're a big girl with big ideas. You got rid of
             that signet ring, didn't you? You knew it was
             dynamite so you got rid of it!
MAVIS: I – I don't know what you're talking about!
TEMPLE: I think you do.
WAITER: Excuse me, sir!
TEMPLE: Yes – what is it?
WAITER: You're wanted on the telephone, Mr Temple.
TEMPLE: Oh, thanks. I'll see you later, Mrs Russell.
MAVIS: I hope so
TEMPLE: (*An afterthought*) Don't get too lonely!

MAVIS: Bobby! Another scotch and martini!
FADE SCENE.

FADE UP.
WAITER: You can take the call in the box over here, sir.
TEMPLE: Thank you.
TEMPLE enters the telephone box and lifts the receiver.
TEMPLE: (*On the phone*) Hello?
OPERATOR: Mr Temple?
TEMPLE: Yes …
OPERATOR: Hold on a moment, please.
We hear the sound of voices on the exchange.
OPERATOR: (*To RICHARD*) Your party's on the line now –
            go ahead, please.
RICHARD: (*On the other end of the line*) Hello?
TEMPLE: Hello?
RICHARD: Paul Temple?
TEMPLE: Yes …
RICHARD: This is Richard Ferguson …
TEMPLE: Oh. I was wondering if I should hear from you!
RICHARD: (*Tensely*) Temple, listen – how's Mrs Gulliver?
TEMPLE: She's ill – very ill.
RICHARD: I was sorry to hear about that, terribly sorry;
            please believe me I …
TEMPLE: (*Quite tough*) Listen, Ferguson – what is it you
            want?
RICHARD: Did you give Mrs Gulliver the ring?
TEMPLE: No, I didn't. I've still got it.
RICHARD: Temple, I've got to have that ring! It's
            important – I've got to have it!
TEMPLE: Well, you know where I am – come and get it.
RICHARD: No, I can't do that. Listen – I'll tell you what
            I'll do …

TEMPLE: (*Tough*) I'll tell you what I'll do, Ferguson! I'll give you twenty minutes. If I don't see you in twenty minutes I'll take this precious signet ring of yours and toss it into the river!

RICHARD: No! Don't do that! Don't do that for … (*Desperately*) Temple, I'll tell you everything, but … Look! Do you know the first AA Box on the Bedford Road? Coming out of Oxford it's on the right – just near a clump of birch trees.

TEMPLE: Yes, I know the one you mean …

RICHARD: I'll be there in fifteen minutes. I'll park my car on the right – near the trees. The car's a black saloon – I'll be sitting in the car – waiting for you.

TEMPLE: Yes, all right, Ferguson. I'll be there. I'll be there in twenty minutes.

TEMPLE replaces the receiver.
FADE SCENE.
FADE UP of music.

FADE DOWN of music.
FADE UP the sound of TEMPLE's car. It is cruising at about forty miles an hour. It slows down during the following scene.

STEVE: We should be very nearly there, darling – surely?

TEMPLE: Yes. I think it's about another quarter of a mile.

A pause.

STEVE: It's awfully dark tonight – isn't it?

TEMPLE: Yes …

STEVE: Slow down, Paul …

TEMPLE: These lights aren't very good, Steve.

STEVE: I know. (*A pause*) I think this is it, Paul.

TEMPLE: Yes, it is. I was wrong. We've just passed the box.

115

The car slows down to almost a standstill.

TEMPLE: There are the trees, over there …

STEVE: I don't see any sign of the car …

TEMPLE: No. (*Suddenly*) Wait a minute! There it is!

TEMPLE pulls up.

TEMPLE: He's parked in the side, near the hedge. His lights are out …

STEVE: Oh, yes. (*A moment*) Have you got the ring?

TEMPLE: Yes, I've got it. But young Ferguson isn't having it, not until I know what this is all about.

TEMPLE opens the car door.

TEMPLE: Stay here, darling. I'll bring him back to the car.

STEVE: No, I'm coming with you!

TEMPLE: Don't be silly …

STEVE: I'm coming with you, Paul!

TEMPLE: All right. Switch the lights off.

STEVE: Why?

TEMPLE: I don't want him to see us – not until we're on top of him.

STEVE: He'll have seen the car …

TEMPLE: That doesn't matter. I don't want him to see us.

TEMPLE and STEVE climb out of the car.

FADE UP of their footsteps.

A pause.

STEVE: He must have seen us by now, Paul!

TEMPLE: Yes. He's getting out of the car.

We hear the sound of the other car's door opening.

MARK: (*Tensely*) You asked for this, my friend – and now you're going to get it!

TEMPLE: Look out, Steve – he's got a revolver!

STEVE: Paul, it's Mark Elliot!

Dramatic FADE UP of music.

END OF EPISODE FOUR

EPISODE FIVE

CONCERNING
RICHARD FERGUSON

OPEN TO:

FADE UP of footsteps.

STEVE: He must have seen us by now, Paul!

TEMPLE: Yes. He's getting out of the car.

We hear the sound of the other car's door opening.

MARK: (*Tensely*) You asked for this, my friend – and
            now you're going to get it!

TEMPLE: Look out, Steve – he's got a revolver!

STEVE: Paul, it's Mark Elliot!

MARK: Temple! Why I thought – I thought …

TEMPLE: Well, what did you think, Elliot?

MARK: I thought you were someone else! I was sure
            that you were … (*Apologetically*) Mrs Temple!
            I'm terribly sorry frightening you like that!

TEMPLE: Is that revolver loaded?

MARK: Yes.

TEMPLE: Who were you expecting?

MARK: I'm sorry, Temple – I can't tell you.

TEMPLE: Was it Richard Ferguson?

MARK: (*Surprised*) Yes, how did you know?

TEMPLE: You're not the only one who has an
            appointment with him.

MARK: You mean you've come here to meet him?

TEMPLE: Yes, but whether he'll turn up is another
            matter.

MARK: But Temple, I can't believe you had an
            appointment with him tonight. You knew that
            sooner or later I should see young Ferguson
            and you deliberately followed me …

STEVE: That's not true, Mr Elliot!

TEMPLE: (*With authority*) I had a phone call from him
            tonight – at your restaurant. I promised to meet

	him here and give him this signet ring – that was about twenty minutes ago.
MARK:	(*Still tense*) Why does he want the ring?
TEMPLE:	Your guess is as good as mine. It might even be better.

A moment.

MARK:	Is that the truth?
TEMPLE:	Yes.
MARK:	I'm sorry. I'm sorry I was rude just now. I … (*Overwrought*) Quite frankly this business has upset me: I've been terribly worried.
TEMPLE:	What business?
MARK:	I told you. Ferguson's blackmailing me. Why, only this morning he … Look here, Temple, we can't talk standing about like this. Let's get into the car.
STEVE:	Let's go back to our car, Paul. I've left my handbag there.
TEMPLE:	Yes, all right, Steve. Come along, Elliot!
MARK:	Temple, what did Ferguson actually say to you when he spoke to you on the phone?

COMPLETE FADE.

FADE UP of MARK ELLIOT speaking.
TEMPLE, STEVE and ELLIOT are sitting in TEMPLE's car.

MARK:	… But that's an amazing story, Temple. You mean to say that Mrs Gulliver – Ferguson's landlady – was actually beaten up.
TEMPLE:	I do.
MARK:	But why?
TEMPLE:	Because someone was under the impression that she had the ring.
MARK:	That sounds incredible! It's like something out of a novel! I just can't believe it.

TEMPLE: Nevertheless, it's true. Now tell me: did you intend to kill Ferguson?

MARK: (*Confused: tense*) I don't know what I intended to do. I certainly didn't intend to give the young swine any more money. I thought perhaps if I threatened him he'd come to his senses and …

STEVE: Mr Elliot, when did Ferguson first start to blackmail you?

MARK: About six or seven weeks ago. You see, I … (*Hesitating*) Well – I suppose I'd better tell you the truth. It all started at a party. One evening – I think it was about the last week in March – I went to a cocktail party given by Mavis Russell. She is quite a personality in Oxford and she'd invited a lot of university people. When I arrived a young man called Rudolf Charles was playing the piano …

COMPLETE FADE.

FADE IN a background of general party conversation and laughter.

FADE UP the piano being played by RUDOLF CHARLES.

PEGGY: Rudolf, what is that thing you're playing?

CHARLES: I'll give you a clue. It's Mendelssohn.

A pause.

PEGGY: Oh, of course I remember! It's one of the Songs without Words.

CHARLES: Clever girl!

PEGGY laughs.

MAVIS: (*Rather keyed up: the hostess*) Darling, must you keep sitting at the piano! (*Raising her voice*) Edward, see to the drinks, I'm sure everybody's dying of thirst.

123

EDWARD: Yes, madam.

The piano stops.

CHARLES: Mavis, you're a bitter disappointment to me. I always thought you had an ear for music.

MAVIS: I have, darling – and you play like an angel, but I want you to meet people. (*Suddenly*) Hello, Mark! How nice to see you!

MARK: My dear, I've been here for twenty minutes. I'm looking for a light sherry and a very pretty girl in a green dress.

MAVIS: Well, we can certainly get you the sherry. (*Raising her voice*) Edward!

CHARLES: It's all right, Mavis. I'll see to it.

MAVIS: Thank you, darling.

FADE conversation down slightly.

MARK: (*A note of seriousness*) I don't see any sign of your protégé, Mavis.

MAVIS: I suppose you mean Richard Ferguson?

MARK: I do.

MAVIS: He hasn't arrived yet. And, Mark, he isn't my protégé. I've told you that before. I encourage him because – well – because I think he's got something.

MARK: Oh he has. He unquestionably has; he's got a confounded cheek.

MAVIS: Why do you say that?

MARK: He phoned me this morning and said he wanted to see me. When I said I couldn't see him – not for a day or two at any rate – he got quite impertinent.

MAVIS: Richard's young and impetuous.

MARK: He's also extremely ill mannered. What is it he wants to see me about, do you know?

124

MAVIS:	Yes. He wants an introduction to a man called Wallace Kean.
MARK:	The publisher?
MAVIS:	Yes. He's a friend of yours, isn't he?
MARK:	He is, and I should like him to remain one.
MAVIS:	(*Pleasantly: interrupting MARK*) Ah, here's Richard now!
RICHARD:	(*Full of apologies; with charm*) Mavis, my sweet, I'm terribly sorry I'm late. We had an awful time getting here and one of the … Oh, I've brought Dinah along. You don't mind, do you, darling? We're having dinner together so it seemed silly for us to …
MAVIS:	No, of course not, I'm delighted. What would you like to drink, Miss – er – ?
DINAH:	Nelson.
MAVIS:	Oh yes, Miss Nelson.
DINAH:	May I have a gin and tonic?
MAVIS:	Yes, of course.
CHARLES:	(*Arriving with a drink*) Here we are, sir. One light sherry! I may not be a very good pianist, Mavis, but I'm certainly the best … Oh, hello. Richard!
RICHARD:	Hello, Rudolf! You know Dinah, of course?
CHARLES:	Yes, of course!
MAVIS:	Oh, I'm sorry! Miss – er?
DINAH:	Nelson.
MAVIS:	Oh yes! Miss Nelson – Mark Elliot.
MARK:	How do you do?
DINAH:	How do you do?
MAVIS:	Mark, you don't look very happy with that sherry!
MARK:	I'm perfectly happy!
EDWARD:	Excuse me, madam …

125

MAVIS:	Yes – what is it?
EDWARD:	Mr Elliot's wanted on the telephone, madam. I've switched it through to the study.
MAVIS:	Oh, thank you, Edward. Do you know where it is, Mark?
MARK:	No, I'm afraid I don't.
RICHARD:	It's all right, I'll show you. I shan't be a moment, Dinah.
DINAH:	Yes, all right, Richard.
RICHARD:	This way, Mr Elliot.

FADE UP of general conversation.

FADE DOWN slightly.
The study door opens.
MARK ELLIOT and RICHARD enter the study.
The study door closes, completely shutting out the noise of the cocktail party.

MARK:	Thank you. Ferguson.
RICHARD:	Not at all.
MARK:	(*Looking round*) Where's the phone?
RICHARD:	(*Casually*) It's over there – in the corner. But I shouldn't bother with it if I were you.
MARK:	What do you mean?
RICHARD:	I asked Edward to give you that message.
MARK:	You asked … Do you mean to say that I'm not wanted on the telephone?
RICHARD:	Sit down, Mr Elliot.
MARK:	What do you mean – sit down?
RICHARD:	It's a perfectly simple statement. Sit down. I want to talk to you.
MARK:	(*Angrily*) Now look here, young man. If you think these block-busting tactics of yours are going to get you anywhere you're very much mistaken!

126

RICHARD: (*Completely unperturbed*) Mr Elliot, you are being aggressive and unfriendly. I want to have a talk with you – a pleasant talk, I hope. This isn't a very good beginning.

MARK: If you think I'm going to introduce you to Wallace Kean you're very much mistaken!

RICHARD: I can't think of anything more boring than having to meet Mr Kean – except possibly having to read one of his books.

MARK: (*Surprised*) But Mavis said you …

RICHARD: I couldn't care less whether I met Mr Kean or not – and that goes for the rest of your distinguished friends.

MARK: Well – what is it you want?

RICHARD: (*Quite simply*) Fifteen hundred pounds.

MARK: I beg your pardon?

RICHARD: I said – fifteen hundred pounds.

MARK: (*Amazed*) You want me to lend you fifteen hundred pounds?

RICHARD: I don't want you to lend me anything. I want you to give me fifteen hundred pounds.

MARK: Give you … (*Laughing*) My dear boy, you're crazy! (*Dismissing the whole matter*) Come along, don't let's waste any more time! Let's go back to the party …

RICHARD: (*Stopping him*) Mr Elliot …

MARK: (*Turning*) Well?

RICHARD: If this was in a book written by Mavis and published by your friend Mr Kean, sooner or later I would find myself saying – "Blackmail is a very ugly word, Mr Elliot." Well, just between ourselves, I don't think it's an ugly word at all. I think it's rather a delightful word – it gets straight to the point. In short, I'm blackmailing you. I want fifteen hundred pounds.

A moment.

MARK: (*Curious*) And supposing I refuse?

RICHARD: Do you remember a girl called Cynthia Stephens? Just in case you don't – let me refresh your memory. Fifteen years ago – you were invited to a house party in Norfolk. A girl – a very young girl – called Cynthia Stephens was also invited. During the course of what I should imagine was an uneventful weekend, Miss Stephens committed suicide. At the inquest you said that she was a comparative stranger: that you'd actually met her, for the first time, that weekend.

MARK: Well?

RICHARD: That wasn't true. You'd met her several times before. On one occasion you'd even taken her over to Brussels for two or three days.

MARK: (*Obviously worried but trying to dismiss the matter*) Quite frankly, I don't know what you're talking about. I vaguely remember a girl called Cynthia Stephens but it's a long time ago. I was very young then and …

RICHARD: You were thirty-one. Miss Stephens was seventeen – sweet seventeen.

A moment.

MARK: I suppose you've got the letters?

RICHARD: I've got three letters. I don't know whether you wrote any more or not.

Another pause.

MARK: (*Quietly: obviously having made up his mind to pay*) You want fifteen hundred pounds for them?

RICHARD: I didn't say that.

MARK: (*Puzzled; worried*) What do you mean?

RICHARD: (*Smiling*) I've got the letters – and I want fifteen hundred pounds. That doesn't mean to say I want fifteen hundred pounds for the letters.

MARK: (*Angrily*) Well, what the devil do you want!?

A pause.

RICHARD: (*Amused; facing MARK*) Fifteen hundred pounds – to be going on with. (*Brightly*) Think it over, Mr Elliot. Think it over. Now, shall we take your advice and join the party?

RICHARD opens the door and there is an immediate sound of laughter and general conversation.

RICHARD: My word, it does sound gay, doesn't it? I'll get you a light sherry – or would you prefer something stronger?

FADE UP of party noises and conversation.
FADE SCENE.

FADE IN of MARK ELLIOT. MARK is in TEMPLE's car, continuing his story.

MARK: …I paid Ferguson the fifteen hundred pounds. Three weeks later I paid him another hundred.

STEVE: How do you know that he has the letters – has he shown them to you?

MARK: He's got them all right …

TEMPLE: What happened today, Elliot – did he phone you?

MARK: Yes. I was in Town. He phoned me about three o'clock. He said he was desperate – that he needed seven hundred pounds. He told me to meet him here – tonight – at nine o'clock. (*Tensely*) Frankly, Temple, I'm not used to this

129

	sort of thing. I – I just don't know how to cope with it.
TEMPLE:	You seemed to be coping with it rather well.
MARK:	What do you mean?
TEMPLE:	Judging by the revolver you'd obviously made up your mind to take care of young Ferguson.
MARK:	I – I must have been crazy! I must have been out of my mind to even think of such a thing! But, Temple, I've got to get those letters back! What am I going to do?
TEMPLE:	Well, I don't think you're going to get them back tonight. It's a quarter past eleven already.
STEVE:	Mr Elliot, you say Richard phoned you this afternoon and arranged to meet you here?
MARK:	Yes.
STEVE:	Then how do you account for the fact that he asked us to meet him here at the same time?
MARK:	I can't account for it, Mrs Temple.
STEVE:	Oh, we know why he phoned us – he wants the ring. It's simply a question of why he picked this particular place at this particular time.
MARK:	(*Tense; obviously under an emotional strain*) I – I can't imagine why.
TEMPLE:	Yes – well, he's obviously not going to keep the appointment. I think it's about time we made a move, Steve.
MARK:	Temple, would you mind driving me back into Oxford? I really don't feel like driving and …
TEMPLE:	Yes, certainly – but what about your car?
MARK:	I'll get my chauffeur to pick it up tomorrow morning. It'll be all right – it's not actually parked on the road.
TEMPLE:	Yes, all right, Elliot.
MARK:	Thank you, Temple. Thank you very much.

130

TEMPLE stars the car: revs up the engine.
FADE SCENE.

FADE UP the sound of TEMPLE's car: it is cruising at about forty miles an hour.

STEVE: Slow down, Paul. I think we're coming to the crossroads.

MARK: No, it's about another quarter of a mile, Mrs Temple.

A pause.

TEMPLE: (*Thoughtfully*) Elliot … the night we first met – at The Encounter – you told me that Richard was blackmailing you and you inferred that Mrs Russell knew all about it.

MARK: I did?

TEMPLE: Yes. You said you had a motive for murdering young Ferguson and when I asked you what that motive was you said – "Do you mean to tell me that Mavis Russell hasn't told you?"

MARK: I'm sorry I said that because I don't really think it was true.

TEMPLE: You mean – you don't think that Mrs Russell did know that you were being blackmailed?

MARK: It's difficult to say. Mavis knows a great deal of what goes on in Oxford – at least what goes on in our particular circle. She may know that I'm being blackmailed but probably thinks young Ferguson's simply – well – putting pressure on me. Ferguson's a careerist, you know. He likes to think that … (*He stops; surprised*) Hello! What's happened here?

STEVE: Slow down, Paul! There's been an accident by the look of things!

The car slows down.

131

TEMPLE: (*Suddenly*) By Timothy, look!

STEVE: That car's on fire!

TEMPLE's car gradually slows down to almost a standstill.

MARK: The police are here, Temple! I wonder what's happened!

We hear the sound of an approaching fire engine.

TEMPLE: (*Out of the car window; calling*) What's happened? My name's Paul Temple.

OFFICER: Oh, good evening, Mr Temple! We don't know, sir! It rather looks as if the petrol tank exploded, sir.

TEMPLE: Is there anyone in the car?

OFFICER: Yes – I'm afraid there is, sir! We've been trying to get him out but we can't get near enough …

FADE UP of FIREMEN taking command of the situation: the sound of voices: men issuing instructions.

TEMPLE: (*Suddenly*) Wait a minute!

STEVE: What is it, Paul?

TEMPLE: (*Getting out of the car*) I want to have a look at the car.

We hear the sound of the car door closing.

MARK: Just look at those fellows! I don't know how the devil they do it!

FIREMAN: (*Shouting*) Stand back over there! Please stand back over there!

We hear the sound of gushing water from a water tank.

MARK: The heat must be terrific!

STEVE: Yes, awful.

MARK switches off the car engine.

FIREMAN: (*Shouting*) Keep it steady!

FADE UP the noise of gushing water and excited voices.

There is the noise of a sudden explosion.

STEVE: (*Startled*) What was that!?

MARK:	The petrol tank, I should think.
STEVE:	Where's Paul?
MARK:	Here he is!
TEMPLE:	(*A note of excitement in his voice*) Get out of the car, Elliot. I want you a moment.
STEVE:	Darling, what is it?
TEMPLE:	It's young Ferguson's car.
MARK:	What!
TEMPLE:	I tell you, it's Ferguson's car! I've checked the number – it's the one he gave me on the phone.
MARK:	(*Nervously*) What do you want me to do?
TEMPLE:	There's a man in that car, Elliot. When they get him out I want you to take a look at him!

ELLIOT gets out of the car.

The car door closes.

Slowly FADE UP the sound of the burning car: excited voices: gushing water, etc.

Pause.

FIREMAN:	All right, boys! Take it steady!
TEMPLE:	They're getting him out …
MARK:	Yes …

A pause.

FIREMAN:	(*Shouting*) Stand back over there! Please stand back! You must stand clear of the car.

FADE UP the sound of burning car.

REGGIE:	Excuse me – isn't it Mr Temple?
TEMPLE:	Why, hello, Mackintosh! What are you doing here?
REGGIE:	Well, I'm supposed to be on my way back to London, but – this held me up!
MARK:	It's a nasty business!
REGGIE:	Yes, it is indeed! It's a very nasty business. I don't see how it happened. The petrol tank

133

couldn't have been the cause of it because we heard it blow up a few moments ago.

There is a sudden gasp from the onlookers.

MARK: Now, what's happening?

TEMPLE: They've got him out of the car!

REGGIE: Aye – poor devil!

FADE UP of the general excitement amongst the crowd.

TEMPLE: Come along, Elliot – you'd better come too, Mackintosh.

REGGIE: What do you mean?

TEMPLE: I want you both to take a good look at this man. I've got a hunch you'll recognise him.

REGGIE: Recognise him! What on earth does he mean, Mr Elliot?

FADE UP the sound of voices and the noise of the burning car.

TEMPLE: (*Pushing his way through the crowd*) Excuse me, please!

FIREMAN: I'm sorry, sir – you can't come through here.

OFFICER: That's all right, George! (*To TEMPLE*) I'm afraid we were too late, Mr Temple. He's dead.

TEMPLE: Oh. (*Quietly*) I want these two gentlemen to take a look at him …

OFFICER: Yes, all right.

FIREMAN: (*Shouting*) We'll have the road cleared in about five minutes! Now please stand back …

A moment.

OFFICER: There you are, sir!

REGGIE: (*Softly: astonished*) Oh, my God!

MARK: You were right, Temple!

TEMPLE: Do you recognise him, Mackintosh?

REGGIE: Why yes, of course! It's Richard Ferguson!

Quiet FADE UP the noise of the burning car.

FADE DOWN the noise of the burning car to the background.

REGGIE: Goodnight, Mr Temple! If you want to get in touch with me I shall be at the same hotel – The Cromwell.

TEMPLE: I thought you were going back to London?

REGGIE: (*Subdued; obviously upset*) I was, but – I've changed my mind. I don't want Dinah to hear about this from anyone else. She was very fond of Richard. This is going to be a blow.

OFFICER: Excuse me, sir.

MARK: Yes?

OFFICER: You're quite certain that it is Richard Ferguson?

MARK: Quite certain. There's no mistake this time.

REGGIE: There's no doubt about it, officer.

OFFICER: Thank you, sir. (*To TEMPLE*) May I have a word with you, Mr Temple?

TEMPLE: Yes, of course. I'll see you at the car, Elliot.

MARK: Yes, all right.

REGGIE: Goodnight.

TEMPLE: Goodnight, Mr Mackintosh.

A pause.

OFFICER: Mr Temple, Ferguson was dead before the car caught fire, sir.

TEMPLE: What do you mean?

OFFICER: I've just taken another look at the body, sir. He was shot …

Dramatic FADE UP of music.

FADE DOWN of music.

FADE IN the voice of MAVIS RUSSELL.

MAVIS: (*Very annoyed*) My dear Sir Graham, I came to this ghastly little police station because I was under the impression that I might be of some help.

FORBES: You certainly can be of some help, Mrs Russell – by answering my questions.

MAVIS: But you keep asking me the same question over and over again! I've told you. I haven't the slightest idea why Richard Ferguson wanted the signet ring.

FORBES: I see.

TEMPLE: (*Quietly*) Mrs Russell, do you mind if I ask you a question? (*A moment*) Did you know that Mr Elliot was being blackmailed by Richard Ferguson?

MAVIS: (*Astounded*) Mark being blackmailed by …? (*Laughing*) Don't be absurd!

TEMPLE: What do you mean?

MAVIS: Have you met Mark Elliot?

TEMPLE: You know I have.

MAVIS: Well, does he strike you as being the sort of man who would let himself be blackmailed by a student? Mark's a shrewd, cool, calculating business man – he wouldn't be blackmailed by anybody. But he might do a spot of it himself.

TEMPLE: Supposing it was Elliot who told me that he was being blackmailed; that he also told me you knew that he was being blackmailed?

MAVIS: Then I should say that he was not only a cool calculating business man but a cool calculating liar. (*Dismissing the whole subject*) It's a quarter past four, Sir Graham. I have an appointment with my hairdresser at half-past. I should rather like to keep it.

FORBES: (*Rising*) Yes, all right, Mrs Russell. I suppose we know where to get in touch with you?

136

MAVIS: You do indeed.

MAVIS opens the door.

MAVIS: Goodbye, Mr Temple. I'm sorry you've been
           so badly misinformed.

TEMPLE: I'll try and make up for it.

The door closes.

A moment.

The door opens and closes.

FORBES: (*Irritable*) I don't like that woman! If she's an
           intellectual, thank heavens I didn't marry one!

TEMPLE: (*Laughing*) The main thing is not to underrate
           her.

FORBES: Temple, do you think she's mixed up in this
           business? I mean really mixed up in it?

TEMPLE: Yes, I do.

FORBES: You don't think that she's Jonathan?

There is a knock and the door opens.

TEMPLE: Well, she could be, Sir Graham. On the other
           hand … (*He stops*)

FORBES: Yes – what is it, sergeant?

SERGEANT: Mr and Mrs Ferguson are here, sir. They're in
           the Inspector's office.

FORBES: All right, sergeant. We'll come down.

SERGEANT: Very good, sir.

FORBES: Come along, Temple!

FADE SCENE.

FADE IN HELEN.

HELEN: (*Obviously distressed and faintly overwrought*)
           … I don't believe it! I don't believe that
           Richard was mixed up in anything that … was
           … dishonest. I knew my own son. He may have
           been impetuous, but … (*She is distressed*)

ROBERT: Helen, please!

137

FORBES: I know this is very painful for you, Mrs Ferguson, but I'm afraid you've got to face the facts, and the facts are not very pleasant. I suppose you've read the report in the newspapers about the car accident?

ROBERT: Yes.

FORBES: Well, it wasn't an accident.

ROBERT: We rather gathered that from what the Inspector said.

FORBES: Your son was shot.

ROBERT: Shot!

HELEN: Oh, no!

FORBES: I'm afraid it's true. According to our medical report he was shot before the car was set on fire. Whether the person who shot him started the fire – we don't know.

ROBERT: (*Exasperated*) Of course the fire was started by the same person – he wanted the whole thing to look like an accident! Sir Graham, I don't want to be offensive but I don't think you people have been too bright over this business.

FORBES: (*Drily*) Really?

ROBERT: Well, when you discovered that Richard wasn't murdered – I mean in the first place – you ought to have picked him up. You ought to have had every cop in town on the look-out for him!

FORBES: But we did! We tried to pick him up!

TEMPLE: Don't forget the police thought Richard was dead. You thought so too, Ferguson: you refused to believe that he was alive even when your wife saw him.

ROBERT: Yeah, I know that, but – Look, Temple, let's have our cards on the table. What's this

	business all about? Why was our boy murdered?
FORBES:	Well, in my opinion, he was murdered because someone was under the impression that he had the signet ring.
HELEN:	The signet ring?
FORBES:	Yes.
ROBERT:	You mean – his own ring?
FORBES:	Yes.
ROBERT:	But why shouldn't he have it? I don't get this! I think you guys are barking up the wrong tree. I think there's a girl mixed up in this somewhere …
HELEN:	Yes, I think so too, Mr Temple. A little while ago Richard wrote us a letter about a girl called Dinah Nelson. He appeared to be very friendly with her.
TEMPLE:	Yes, I think he was.
FORBES:	Haven't you met Miss Nelson?
HELEN:	No, we haven't.
ROBERT:	And then there's this other woman – this Mrs Russell. Do you think she knows anything about this?
FORBES:	Yes, it's possible.
ROBERT:	(*Exasperated*) Well, why don't you get her down here!? Why don't you question her?
FORBES:	We have questioned her: she left here only a few minutes ago. (*Briskly*) Mr Ferguson – I want you to take a look at this –
HELEN:	What is it?
FORBES:	Take a look at it. (*A moment*) It's a photostatic copy of a message that was on the first Jonathan card.

Slight pause.

HELEN: What is it?
ROBERT: It's just a list of letters and numbers so far as I can see. Is this supposed to mean something?
FORBES: Let Mrs Ferguson have a look at it.
HELEN: (*Taking the card*) Thank you.
A pause.
FORBES: Well – does that make sense to you?
ROBERT: Not to me it doesn't!
HELEN: I've certainly never seen anything like this before.
FORBES: (*Taking back the card*) I see. Now, Mrs Ferguson, tell me: when was the last time you saw your son?
HELEN: Why, that night. The night I saw him standing outside of the hotel.
FORBES: You've … never seen him since?
HELEN: No.
FORBES: You know that he telephoned your husband one night and asked him to meet him at a house in Lewisham?
HELEN: Yes, Robert told me.
FORBES: Were you surprised?
HELEN: Yes, of course I was!
ROBERT: Say, what is this?
FORBES: (*Ignoring ROBERT's remark*) Mr Ferguson had a heart attack and was unable to keep the appointment. Mr Temple kept it. But instead of seeing your son he found the dead body of a man called Red Harris.
HELEN: Yes, I know.
FORBES: Have you ever heard of Red Harris?
HELEN: No, never.

FORBES: So, in spite of the fact that he telephoned your husband, Richard made no attempt to get in touch with you, Mrs Ferguson?

HELEN: No, he didn't.

FORBES: I see. (*Dismissing the FERGUSONS*) Well, thank you both. We'll be in touch with you. If anything important develops we'll most certainly let you know.

ROBERT: We thought of going back to London tonight – is that o.k.?

FORBES: Yes. I take it you're still at the same hotel?

ROBERT: Yeah – for the time being at any rate. Goodbye, Temple.

TEMPLE: Goodbye, Mr Ferguson. Goodbye, Mrs Ferguson.

FORBES: I'll be back in a moment, Temple!

The door opens and closes.

A pause.

The door opens again.

TEMPLE: Oh, hello, Mrs Ferguson.

HELEN: Excuse me. I think I left my handbag.

TEMPLE: Your handbag? Oh, here it is.

HELEN: Thank you. (*A moment*) Mr Temple …

TEMPLE: Yes?

HELEN: (*A whisper*) Get in touch with Dinah Nelson. Tell her I sent you …

The door closes.

FADE UP of music.

FADE DOWN of music.

Slow FADE IN of street noises. There is a background of traffic sounds.

TEMPLE and STEVE are walking along the pavement.

STEVE:	Did you tell Sir Graham what Mrs Ferguson said?
TEMPLE:	No, I didn't.
STEVE:	But it doesn't make sense, does it? First of all she said she didn't know Dinah Nelson and then later she said – get in touch with her and tell her she sent you.
TEMPLE:	Yes.
STEVE:	Well, why on earth do you think she said that?
TEMPLE:	I don't know. (*Suddenly*) Hello, this looks like the place! Weldon Court …
STEVE:	M'm … looks impressive.
TEMPLE:	Yes, it does, doesn't it?

FADE SCENE.

CROSS FADE to the inside of Weldon Court.
FADE IN of STEVE.

STEVE:	It's rather a splendid hall, Paul.
TEMPLE:	Yes. Quite luxurious.
STEVE:	Isn't Dinah Nelson secretary to Professor Dilwright?
TEMPLE:	Yes.
STEVE:	Well, I shouldn't think she lives here on her salary – she must have private means.
TEMPLE:	Yes, I should imagine so.
PORTER:	Good evening, sir. Can I help you?
TEMPLE:	Miss Nelson – is that number 3?
PORTER:	Yes, sir. Flat 3. First floor.
TEMPLE:	Thank you. Do you happen to know if Miss Nelson is in?
PORTER:	Yes, she is, sir. She came in about a quarter past seven. I should take the lift, sir.

The PORTER opens the lift gate.

PORTER:	Allow me, madam …

STEVE: (*Entering the lift*) Thank you.

PORTER: Thank you, madam.

The lift gates close.

A slight pause.

The lift starts to ascend.

The lift stops.

The lift gates are opened and closed.

A pause.

TEMPLE: This is three …

TEMPLE presses the bell push. We hear the bell.

STEVE: Yes, it certainly has an expensive look. (*Pause*) Just the two flats on each floor.

TEMPLE: Um. The rents must be pretty steep.

STEVE: Yes.

TEMPLE: As you said, she couldn't live here just on her salary.

STEVE: No.

A pause.

STEVE: I should ring again, Paul.

TEMPLE rings the bell again.

A long pause.

TEMPLE rings again.

A pause.

STEVE: She can't be in.

TEMPLE rings the bell again.

TEMPLE: M-m – it doesn't look like it. (*A slight pause*) The porter must have been mistaken. She's probably gone … (*He stops*)

STEVE: What is it?

TEMPLE: Do you smell anything?

STEVE: (*Sniffing*) It's gas!

TEMPLE: Yes!

STEVE: (*Quickly*) What are you doing?

TEMPLE: (*Quickly; tensely*) The key's in the lock!

143

STEVE: Paul, you don't think she's tried to commit
            suicide?
TEMPLE: I do! Hold this newspaper, Steve! That's right.
            Now spread it out on the floor …
STEVE: What are you going to do?
TEMPLE: I'm going to put it under the door and try to get
            the key to fall on it.
STEVE: I'll do it …

STEVE pushes the paper under the door.

TEMPLE: That's it … Steady … Keep it flat …
STEVE: It's under …
TEMPLE: Right!

*TEMPLE bangs the door with his fist – a sharp bang – and
we hear the key fall out of the lock on to the newspaper.*

STEVE: You've done it!
TEMPLE: Pull the paper out – from under the door.
            Gently, Steve …

STEVE is pulling the newspaper from under the door.

TEMPLE: Not too fast … Careful.
STEVE: I've got it.
TEMPLE: Good.

TEMPLE unlocks the door and throws it open.

STEVE: (*Coughing*) Oh, Paul! (*She is gasping for
            breath*)
TEMPLE: (*Gasping*) Stay where you are, Steve!
STEVE: (*Coughing; trying to get her breath*) She's over
            there! Near the gas fire …
TEMPLE: I'll open the window …

TEMPLE crosses the room and throws open the window.

STEVE: I've turned off the gas.

*TEMPLE and STEVE are both coughing and gasping for
breath.*

TEMPLE: Help me to get her over to the window …
STEVE: Is she all right?

TEMPLE:	I don't know … (*Holding DINAH; shaking her slightly*) Miss Nelson … Miss Nelson …
STEVE:	Careful, you'll hurt her.
TEMPLE:	I've got to get her … (*Struggling to move DINAH*) … near … the … window …
STEVE:	It's beginning to clear …
TEMPLE:	(*Holding DINAH*) Miss Nelson … Miss Nelson …
STEVE:	She's coming round!
TEMPLE:	Yes, I think she is …
DINAH:	(*Dazed; bewildered*) Where am I? Where … am … I? What … (*She starts to cough*)
TEMPLE:	It's all right. Now take it easy …
DINAH:	What happened? What … Oh, my head!
TEMPLE:	Now take a deep breath …
DINAH:	I must have fainted, I must … (*Tensely; distressed*) Oh, I remember! I remember now, I tried to … (*She is feeling faint and dizzy*) Everything's going round, Mr Temple … I can't see properly, I feel dizzy …

A pause.

STEVE:	Is she going to be all right, Paul?
TEMPLE:	Yes, she'll be all right. (*Quietly; aside*) Go into the bedroom, Steve – see if she left a note for anyone …
STEVE:	Yes, all right.

A moment.

TEMPLE:	Now relax, Miss Nelson … Just close your eyes … That's it … (*Gently: watching DINAH*)

A pause.

DINAH:	(*With deep, deliberate breathing*) I … I … feel better now …
TEMPLE:	Yes – well, just sit quiet for a moment or so …

145

DINAH: (*Suddenly*) Mr Temple, I tried to commit
            suicide. I made up my mind that I couldn't
            stand … things … any … longer … I … (*She is
            emotional again; near to tears*)
STEVE: (*Calling from the bedroom*) Paul!
TEMPLE: (*Looking up*) Yes?
STEVE: Here a moment …
TEMPLE crosses to STEVE.
A moment.
TEMPLE: What is it, Steve?
STEVE: (*Quietly*) You were right. There is a note. It
            was on the dressing table in the bedroom.
TEMPLE: Well?
STEVE: It's for Jonathan …
FADE UP of music.

END OF EPISODE FIVE

EPISODE SIX

A SURPRISE FOR
MAVIS RUSSELL

OPEN TO:

TEMPLE: Now relax, Miss Nelson … Just close your eyes
            … That's it … (*Gently: watching DINAH*)

A pause.

DINAH: (*With deep, deliberate breathing*) I … I … feel
            better now …

TEMPLE: Yes – well, just sit quiet for a moment or so …

DINAH: (*Suddenly*) Mr Temple, I tried to commit
            suicide. I made up my mind that I couldn't
            stand … things … any … longer … I … (*She is
            emotional again; near to tears*)

STEVE: (*Calling from the bedroom*) Paul!

TEMPLE: (*Looking up*) Yes?

STEVE: Here a moment …

TEMPLE crosses to STEVE.

A moment.

TEMPLE: What is it, Steve?

STEVE: (*Quietly*) You were right. There is a note. It
            was on the dressing table in the bedroom.

TEMPLE: Well?

STEVE: It's for Jonathan …

A moment.

TEMPLE: Jonathan … let me see. (*Reading*) "This is the
            only way out for me. I just can't stand things
            any longer, Dinah …" …

DINAH: (*From the background*) Mr Temple!

TEMPLE: Coming, Miss Nelson!

TEMPLE and STEVE return to DINAH.

DINAH: Could I have a glass of water, please?

TEMPLE: Yes, of course.

STEVE: I'll get it.

DINAH: The kitchen's … on … the … left, Mrs Temple.

TEMPLE: Are you feeling any better?

149

DINAH: I still feel a little sick …
TEMPLE: Yes, of course, but you'll feel all right in a few
            minutes.
DINAH: You … just turned up in time, Mr Temple, I …
            I … (*Suddenly; tensely*) The note! I left a note
            in the bedroom, please get it for me.
TEMPLE: (*Quietly*) It's here …
DINAH: Give it to me! Please!

DINAH snatches the note and tears it up.

TEMPLE: I'm afraid I've already read it.
DINAH: What!
TEMPLE: It's addressed to Jonathan. (*A moment*) Who is
            Jonathan?
DINAH: I … I don't know.
TEMPLE: One doesn't usually leave a suicide note to a
            person one doesn't know.
DINAH: Mr Temple, please don't ask me any questions!
            (*Near to tears*) Please don't.
TEMPLE: I'm afraid I've got to ask you these questions.
            Who is Jonathan, and why did Richard
            Ferguson want the ring?
DINAH: (*Tensely*) I don't know! I tell you I don't know!
            Please leave me alone!
STEVE: Here's some water.
TEMPLE: (*Gently*) Here we are, Dinah. Now, drink this
            …
DINAH: (*Taking a drink*) Thank you. (*She drinks*)

A pause.

TEMPLE: Do you feel better?
DINAH: Yes.
STEVE: I think you'd better go into the bedroom and lie
            down for a little while. If there's anything you
            want we can get it for you.
DINAH: Yes, I'd – I'd like to do that, Mrs Temple.

TEMPLE:	Right. Give me your arm.
DINAH:	(*Faint*) Oh, I do feel weak, I …
TEMPLE:	It's all right, Dinah, don't worry … Go and turn the bed down, Steve. I'll carry her in …

FADE SCENE.

FADE UP of STEVE talking.

STEVE:	How do you feel?
DINAH:	Better, thanks. This hot water bottle's heavenly … It's awfully good of you, Mrs Temple. I do appreciate it.
TEMPLE:	Are you still feeling cold?
DINAH:	Not quite so cold as I was.
TEMPLE:	You know, I still think I ought to get a doctor.
DINAH:	No, please don't! I'll – I'll be all right, honestly I will.
TEMPLE:	All right. Now, Miss Nelson, tell me …
DINAH:	(*Still emotional: she is grateful to TEMPLE and STEVE but still a little frightened of being questioned*) You called me Dinah just now. I wish … you'd both go on calling me Dinah. It's – it's much more friendly.
TEMPLE:	Very well, Dinah. Tell me: do you know why we came here tonight?
DINAH:	No. But – I'm very glad you did.
TEMPLE:	We came because Mrs Ferguson told me to get in touch with you.
DINAH:	(*Tensely*) Mrs Ferguson?
TEMPLE:	Yes.
DINAH:	(*Almost angrily*) Why – why should she do that?
TEMPLE:	Don't you know why?
DINAH:	No, I don't. I – I don't know Mrs Ferguson, I've never even met her.

151

TEMPLE: And you've no idea why she told us to get in touch with you?

DINAH: (*She is near to tears again*) No, I've told you, I haven't.

STEVE: (*Softly: a warning*) Paul …

A pause.

STEVE: Now, Dinah, just relax …

TEMPLE: (*Pleasantly: changing the subject*) Dinah, when was this photograph taken?

DINAH: (*Through her tears*) Which – which one? Oh, that was taken about six months ago.

TEMPLE: It's Richard Ferguson with you, isn't it?

DINAH: Yes. (*A moment: faintly amused*) What are you doing?

TEMPLE: Just looking at the photograph.

DINAH: Yes, I know, but – I didn't know real detectives used magnifying glasses!

STEVE: Invariably. And bloodhounds. We left ours in the hall.

DINAH: (*Gives a little laugh*) Mr Temple, you must have thought me very rude just now and very ungrateful.

TEMPLE: What do you mean?

DINAH: When I refused to answer your questions.

TEMPLE: No, I didn't think you were rude or ungrateful, I just thought you were being rather stupid. (*Friendly*) Miss Nelson …

DINAH: Dinah …

The front door bell rings.

TEMPLE: Look, Dinah, I'm sure I can help you over this business, why don't you let me?

STEVE: It's the front door, Paul.

TEMPLE: Are you expecting anyone?

DINAH: Oh, yes. Yes, I'm expecting Reggie, I ... I
            forgot about that.
TEMPLE: Do you want to see him?
DINAH: (*Tensely*) Yes. Yes, I suppose I'll have to see
            him.

The bell rings again.

TEMPLE: Stay with Dinah, Steve.
STEVE: Yes, all right.

*TEMPLE crosses out of the bedroom and opens the front
door.*

REGGIE: (*Surprised*) Oh! Hello!
TEMPLE: Hello, Mackintosh! Good evening, Mr Charles!
CHARLES: We didn't expect to find you here, Mr Temple!
REGGIE: No! We have a date with Dinah and ...
TEMPLE: You'd better come in.

The door shuts.

CHARLES: There's a strong smell of gas!
REGGIE: (*Anxiously*) Temple, what is it? What's
            happened?
TEMPLE: Your friend Dinah tried to commit suicide ...
CHARLES: What!
REGGIE: No, I don't believe it ...
TEMPLE: I'm afraid it's true.
REGGIE: (*Quickly*) Is she all right?
TEMPLE: Yes, she's all right. There's nothing to worry
            about. Fortunately we arrived in time.
REGGIE: Where is she?
TEMPLE: She's in the bedroom – my wife's with her.
            (*Stopping REGGIE*) Wait a moment,
            Mackintosh! I want to have a word with you.
REGGIE: Are you sure Dinah's all right?
TEMPLE: I've already told you that. There's nothing to
            worry about.

CHARLES: It's a very good thing you turned up when you did, Mr Temple!

TEMPLE: (*Bluntly*) A very good thing, Mr Charles! (*Suddenly; quite friendly*) Incidentally, I didn't know you two knew each other?

CHARLES: We met in a golf tournament about six months ago. We've been firm friends ever since.

TEMPLE: Had you a date with Miss Nelson?

CHARLES: Yes, we'd arranged to take her to The Encounter.

TEMPLE: When did you make the date?

CHARLES: This afternoon.

REGGIE: I telephoned her.

TEMPLE: How did she seem?

REGGIE: Well, she sounded a bit down, I thought. Of course she was terribly upset when she heard about young Ferguson. There's no doubt about it, that's why she tried to commit suicide. I knew all the time that it would be a great …

TEMPLE: (*Interrupting REGGIE*) I don't agree, Mackintosh. I may be wrong – but I don't think young Ferguson's death had anything to do with her attempt to commit suicide.

CHARLES: But what other explanation can there be?

TEMPLE: Miss Nelson left a note – a note addressed to someone called Jonathan.

REGGIE: Jonathan?

CHARLES: I've never heard of anyone called Jonathan.

TEMPLE: Yes – you told me that once before, Mr Charles.

CHARLES: What did the note say?

TEMPLE: It said that she just couldn't stand things any longer.

REGGIE: What things? What did she mean?

TEMPLE:	You'd better ask her yourself. Incidentally, please don't think I'm impertinent, but you seem to see quite a lot of your sister-in-law, don't you, Mackintosh?
REGGIE:	Yes, I've been waiting for you to raise that point. Not that it's any business of yours, mark you. For almost two years after the accident I never went anywhere. I never dined out, I never went to the theatre …
TEMPLE:	What accident?
CHARLES:	Mrs Mackintosh had a motor car accident: she was badly injured. If Reggie didn't take Dinah out occasionally, he'd – well – he just wouldn't go anywhere.
TEMPLE:	I see.
REGGIE:	I hope you do see, Mr Temple. Dinah's a nice girl.

The bedroom door opens.

STEVE:	(*In the bedroom doorway*) Paul!
REGGIE:	Good evening, Mrs Temple!
TEMPLE:	What is it, Steve?
STEVE:	Dinah's asking for Mr Mackintosh.
TEMPLE:	We're just coming.
STEVE:	Paul, she's rather upset again – she's crying.
TEMPLE:	Yes, all right, Steve.

FADE SCENE.

FADE IN of DINAH crying.

| REGGIE: | (*Gently*) Now, Dinah, my dear, don't be silly! There's no need to get upset – no need at all. You did a very silly thing but, thanks to Mr and Mrs Temple, it's turned out for the best. Now just try an' pull yourself together. |

DINAH: (*Distressed*) Reggie, I don't want to answer any questions, I don't … want … to … talk … about … anything.

REGGIE: All right, Dinah. Now just relax.

DINAH: Don't ask me any more questions, Mr Temple. Please don't. I – I can't answer … them … not … tonight.

TEMPLE: We're going back to the hotel, Dinah. If you change your mind and feel like talking – well – you know where to find us.

DINAH: Yes, all right.

REGGIE: Rudolf, I'm staying with Dinah – we'd better forget our dinner date.

CHARLES: Yes, of course, Reggie. Have you got your car, Mr Temple?

TEMPLE: No, as a matter of fact we haven't.

CHARLES: I'll give you a lift back to your hotel.

TEMPLE: Thank you. (*Aside*) Mackintosh, if she changes her mind and decides to talk …

REGGIE: (*Quietly*) I'll be in touch with you straight away – you can depend on it.

TEMPLE: Thank you. (*To STEVE*) Are you ready, Steve?

STEVE: Yes. Good night, Dinah.

DINAH: Good night, Mrs Temple. You may not think so, but – I'm – really terribly grateful to you …

STEVE: Well, take care of yourself and when you feel better give us a ring.

CHARLES: Good night, Dinah!

DINAH: (*Weakly*) Good night …

REGGIE: Now I'll get you a nice cup of tea, Dinah. You'll feel a different girl when you've had a cup of tea.

DINAH: (*Still tense*) No. No, not just now, Reggie, please. Stay with me.

156

REGGIE: (*Consoling DINAH*) Yes, all right, Dinah. Just as you please, my dear. Just as you please …

COMPLETE FADE.

Slow FADE IN the sound of CHARLES's car: it is travelling at an average speed.

TEMPLE: This car runs very smoothly, Charles.

CHARLES: Yes, I'm very pleased with it.

STEVE: What make is it?

CHARLES: It's a Lombard, Mrs Temple. A three and a half litre.

TEMPLE: Oh, a Lombard. (*Takes stock of the car*) Yes, I thought it was. How long have you had it?

CHARLES: (*Hesitating*) About six months.

TEMPLE: I must say, it's extremely comfortable, isn't it, Steve?

STEVE: Yes, very.

TEMPLE: Did you buy it in Oxford?

CHARLES: No, I bought it in London.

TEMPLE: (*Casually*) Second-hand?

CHARLES: Yes, second-hand.

TEMPLE: You don't see many Lombards about, do you? I suppose they're too big for most people. A friend of mine used to have one – a very nice car, too. His name was Red Harris.

CHARLES: (*Completely ignoring the reference to RED HARRIS*) The thing I like about them is the quick get-away, it's absolutely first rate.

TEMPLE: Yes. I say, I hope you won't mind my asking, but – what do you do exactly?

CHARLES: I'm an architect.

TEMPLE: Oh.

STEVE: I thought you were an undergraduate, Mr Charles.

157

CHARLES: I was: I came down two years ago.
CHARLES takes his foot off the accelerator.
CHARLES: Ah, here we are!
TEMPLE: Well, thanks for the lift.
CHARLES: Not at all. I hope Dinah goes on all right.
The car stops.
TEMPLE: Yes, I hope so, too.
CHARLES: I think she will. I should imagine this has taught her a lesson.
STEVE: Have you any idea why she should want to commit suicide?
CHARLES: The only reason I can think of is the one Reggie gave.
TEMPLE: Because of Richard Ferguson?
CHARLES: Yes.
TEMPLE: How well did you know Ferguson?
CHARLES: You've already asked me that question.
TEMPLE: Have I?
CHARLES: Yes, I told you: we met about half a dozen times at cocktail parties and that sort of thing.
TEMPLE: Do you remember a party given by Mavis Russell about – oh, I should say, about seven or eight months ago?
CHARLES: Yes, I remember.
TEMPLE: Richard Ferguson was there.
CHARLES: Was he? It's more than likely.
TEMPLE: Can you remember that party very well?
CHARLES: What is it you want me to remember?
TEMPLE: Do you remember whether Mark Elliot was called to the telephone?
CHARLES: I'm afraid I don't even remember whether Mr Elliot was at the party.
TEMPLE: I see.
Suddenly: we hear the opening of the car door.

TEMPLE: Well, thanks for the lift.

CHARLES: Not at all.

The second door opens.

CHARLES: Good night, Mrs Temple.

The car doors close.

STEVE: Good night.

CHARLES changes gear and quickly accelerates: the car makes a quick getaway.

A pause.

STEVE: You seemed very interested in the car, Paul.

TEMPLE: Yes, I was. Do you know why?

STEVE: No.

TEMPLE: Because I've been in it before, that's why! It's the car that Red Harris had. The car we sat in the night he told me about the ring.

STEVE: You mean the <u>same</u> car?

TEMPLE: The same car! It's a different colour and it's got a different index number but – by Timothy, Steve – it's the same car!

Dramatic FADE UP of music.

FADE DOWN of music.

FADE UP background conversation and the noises of the main hall of the hotel.

PORTER: Good evening, Mr Temple. Good evening, madam!

STEVE: Good evening.

TEMPLE: Could I have my key, please?

PORTER: Yes, certainly, sir. (*Confidentially*) The gentleman in 33 would like to have a word with you, Mr Temple. He's in his room now, sir.

TEMPLE: Oh, thank you.

STEVE: Is that Sir Graham?

TEMPLE:	Yes. (*To the PORTER*) If there are any telephone calls for me in the next half hour or so put them through to room 33.
PORTER:	Very good, sir.
ROBERT:	(*Approaching: calling to TEMPLE and STEVE*) Temple!
TEMPLE:	(*Turning*) Oh, hello, Ferguson!
ROBERT:	(*Agitated*) Temple, could I have a word with you?
TEMPLE:	Yes, of course. Let's go into the lounge, shall we?

FADE the noises of the main hall.

FADE UP.

STEVE:	Is anything wrong, Mr Ferguson?
ROBERT:	(*Tense and agitated*) Well – I don't know, Mrs Temple. I guess I'm just imagining things, at least I hope so.
TEMPLE:	Well, sit down.

A moment.

ROBERT sits down.

TEMPLE:	Now what's it all about?
ROBERT:	Well – Helen – my wife – (*With a nervous little laugh*) She seems to have disappeared.
TEMPLE:	(*Surprised*) Disappeared?
ROBERT:	Yes.
STEVE:	What do you mean?
ROBERT:	Well, this afternoon, just after we left you and Sir Graham at the police station – Helen said she wanted to do some shopping. I guess it would be about – about a quarter past four. Well, I told her to go ahead and said I'd meet her here – at the hotel – at about half past five.
TEMPLE:	Well?

160

ROBERT: Well, I haven't seen her since. It's a quarter to nine and she hasn't turned up.

STEVE: Yes, but surely that doesn't mean she's disappeared. She may have met some friends – or gone to the pictures.

ROBERT: We don't know anyone in Oxford, Mrs Temple – and Helen certainly wouldn't go to a movie on her own.

TEMPLE: Well, I'm sure there's a perfectly simple explanation, Ferguson. I shouldn't worry about it.

ROBERT: (*Worried*) I don't know. Helen's been acting mighty queer just lately, she … well, when she heard about Richard I thought she was going to have a breakdown. A real breakdown, I mean.

TEMPLE: She did seem rather strung up.

ROBERT: I don't like it, Temple. I'm worried.

TEMPLE: Ferguson, when I asked your wife this afternoon if she knew Dinah Nelson, she said that she'd never met her.

ROBERT: That's right.

TEMPLE: Have you met her?

ROBERT: No, I haven't.

TEMPLE: How long ago is it since you saw …

STEVE: (*Interrupting TEMPLE*) Paul, here's Mr Elliot!

MARK: (*Extremely annoyed*) Oh, so here you are, Temple!

TEMPLE: Hello, Elliot!

STEVE: You don't look very pleased with life, Mr Elliot.

MARK: I'm not feeling very pleased with life, Mrs Temple! I'm not very pleased with your husband either!

TEMPLE: Oh? What have I done?

161

MARK:	Last night I told you in strict confidence – about my relationship with Richard Ferguson.
TEMPLE:	Well?
MARK:	(*Angrily*) Well, tonight Mrs Ferguson – Richard's mother – calmly walks into The Encounter, apologises for her son's behaviour, and presents me with a cheque for nineteen hundred pounds!
ROBERT:	(*Amazed*) You mean to say that my wife … I don't get this!
TEMPLE:	You're not the only one, Ferguson!
MARK:	(*Turning on ROBERT*) Are you Richard Ferguson's father?
ROBERT:	I am, sir!
MARK:	(*Angrily*) Then I suppose you're in on this!
TEMPLE:	Just a minute, Elliot! Calm down! (*A moment*) Now let's get this straightened out. In the first place, I did not tell Mrs Ferguson or anyone else that you'd been blackmailed by Richard.
ROBERT:	(*Interrupting TEMPLE: angrily*) What do you mean, blackmailed?
TEMPLE:	According to Mr Elliot your son was a blackmailer. He'd already had nineteen hundred pounds from him.
ROBERT:	(*Interrupting TEMPLE again*) That's a lie!
MARK:	(*Quietly*) I'm afraid it isn't a lie, Mr Ferguson – it's the truth. But now that the boy's dead there's no need to even discuss the matter. It was decent of your wife to offer me the money back but – well, all I want to do about this business is forget it.
ROBERT:	What d'you mean – forget it? Richard was murdered! If this story of yours is true, that

	means you had a motive for murdering him. A pretty good motive!
MARK:	(*Calmly*) I had. But I didn't murder him.
ROBERT:	(*Quietly*) When did you last see my wife?
MARK:	About twenty minutes ago.
ROBERT:	Is she still at The Encounter?
MARK:	As far as I know: she was in the cocktail bar when I left.
ROBERT:	(*Brusquely: leaving*) I'll see you later, Temple!
TEMPLE:	Yes, all right, Ferguson.

A moment.

STEVE:	Mr Elliot, did Mrs Ferguson tell you that it was through my husband that she knew about Richard blackmailing you?
MARK:	No, I'm afraid I assumed that.
TEMPLE:	Well, you were wrong.
MARK:	But if you didn't tell her, Temple – then who did?
TEMPLE:	Yes, – that's quite a question. Who did?

FADE IN of music.

FADE DOWN of music.
Slow FADE IN of Temple speaking:

TEMPLE:	… So if Elliot's telling the truth, then quite obviously someone told Helen Ferguson about Richard, Sir Graham.
FORBES:	M'm. Yes. Where's Ferguson at the moment?
TEMPLE:	He's gone to The Encounter to pick up his wife.
FORBES:	Did he seem very upset when he thought she was missing?
STEVE:	He certainly did!
TEMPLE:	Sir Graham, tell me: is there any news about Mrs Gulliver?

163

FORBES:	Yes, that's one of the things I wanted to see you about. She never regained consciousness: she died this afternoon, Temple.
STEVE:	Oh, poor soul!
TEMPLE:	I'm sorry about that.
FORBES:	Mrs Gulliver was certainly mixed up in this business, but to what extent we don't really know.
STEVE:	Did you check on the car numbers, Sir Graham?
FORBES:	Yes, Steve, I did. And that's really what I wanted to see you about. Here's the copy of the card. Now take a good look at it, Temple. (*Reading*) "789 ALE ..." That's a Passide: it was stolen two weeks ago from a garage in Chelmsford.
TEMPLE:	Go on ...
FORBES:	267 FLO – there's no record of that number at all. 316 FXH – that's an American Bretalac: it was stolen from Grosvenor Square about six weeks ago. 574 DXD – no record. 769 DLC – a Rolls – stolen from a garage in Knightbridge three weeks ago. 902 ALN – no record. (*Looking up*) You see the significance, Temple?
TEMPLE:	I'm beginning to.
STEVE:	You mean the numbers you've got no record of ...
FORBES:	Are the numbers we've got no record of – the phoney numbers – substituted for the genuine ones. In other words 316 FXH becomes 574 DXD and 789 ALE becomes 267 FLO ...

TEMPLE: (*Intrigued*) So that means the postcard was sent to Richard Ferguson so that he'd know which was which …

FORBES: Yes. It's my bet that young Ferguson was in this car racket – in it up to his neck.

STEVE: But, Sir Graham, what about log books? Surely every car has got to have one.

FORBES: If they can forge pound notes and dollars, Steve, they can certainly print log books.

TEMPLE: M'm. Things are beginning to tie up: you remember the car that Red Harris had? It was a Lombard.

FORBES: Yes; you said it was 246 ELF.

TEMPLE: Yes, well it isn't any longer. It belongs to Rudolf Charles. It's been re-sprayed and the number's been changed.

FORBES: Are you sure it's the same car?

TEMPLE: I'd stake my life on it. I felt it the moment I got into the car. There was something about the sunshine roof – it's difficult to explain – but I knew darn well I'd been in that car before.

FORBES: (*Thoughtfully*) M'm. Well, how does the signet ring fit into all this?

TEMPLE: Well, it's my opinion that it was a means of identification.

FORBES: What do you mean?

TEMPLE: You told us that a man called André Dumas was mixed up in the stolen car racket and that he'd been arrested.

FORBES: That's right. The French people have been after him for some time. We first heard of Dumas about six months ago – there was some talk of him coming over here and the Sûreté tipped us off.

165

TEMPLE:	I've been thinking about Dumas. I'm not so sure that he isn't connected with this Jonathan affair in some way or other.
STEVE:	Why do you say that, Paul?
TEMPLE:	Do you remember what was on the signet ring, Steve?
STEVE:	Yes – two letters and two numbers. A4 and D4.
TEMPLE:	Yes, A4 … D4. Well, perhaps it's only a coincidence, but …
FORBES:	I see what you're getting at, Temple. You mean A4 might stand for Andre – A and four letters – Andre. D4 …
STEVE:	D and four letters – Dumas!
TEMPLE:	Yes.
STEVE:	I wonder if you're right?
TEMPLE:	Sir Graham, when I was at Dinah Nelson's I picked up a photograph of Richard Ferguson – according to her it was taken six months ago.
FORBES:	Well?
TEMPLE:	Well, he wasn't wearing a ring.
FORBES:	He wasn't? Are you sure? You can easily be mistaken in a photograph.

The telephone rings.

| TEMPLE: | I wasn't mistaken. I examined the photograph through a magnifying glass. |
| FORBES: | Excuse me. |

FORBES lifts the telephone receiver.

FORBES:	Hello?
PORTER:	There's a call for Mr Temple, sir.
FORBES:	Oh, just a moment. (*To TEMPLE*) It's for you, Temple.
TEMPLE:	Oh, thank you. (*On the phone*) Hello?
PORTER:	(*On the other end of the line*) Just a moment, sir.

166

A moment.

REGGIE: (*On the other end of the line*) Is that you, Mr Temple?

TEMPLE: Oh, hello, Mackintosh! How's Miss Nelson?

REGGIE: She seems to be very much better. Very much better indeed.

TEMPLE: Oh, good. I'm glad to hear that.

REGGIE: As a matter of fact that's why I've telephoned you. (*Quietly; confidentially*) She wants to see you, Mr Temple. I've convinced her that the best thing she can do is have a heart to heart talk with you.

TEMPLE: Good. Are you speaking from her flat?

REGGIE: Yes.

TEMPLE: I'll be with you in about half an hour.

REGGIE: Right. (*Suddenly*) Oh, er – you'll be on your own, I take it?

TEMPLE: Well – except for my wife …

REGGIE: No, I didn't mean that! I mean – you won't bring anyone else along … Sir Graham, for instance?

TEMPLE: No, we'll be on our own.

REGGIE: I think it would be best, if you don't mind.

TEMPLE: I'll see you in thirty minutes.

REGGIE: (*Quite chirpily*) O.K.!

TEMPLE replaces the receiver.

STEVE: What is it, Paul?

TEMPLE: Dinah Nelson wants to see us. According to our friend Mackintosh he's persuaded her to talk …

FORBES: Mackintosh has?

TEMPLE: Yes. (*A moment*) I wonder?

FADE IN of music.

FADE DOWN of music.

167

FADE IN background noises and conversation of the main hall of the hotel.

TEMPLE: Here's my key, porter.
PORTER: Thank you, Mr Temple.
TEMPLE: Will you get me a taxi, please?
PORTER: Very good, sir.
STEVE: What about the car, darling?
TEMPLE: I don't think there's much point in getting the car out, Steve – it only means that … (*Pleasantly*) Why, hello, Mrs Russell!
MAVIS: Hello, Mr Temple! Good evening, Mrs Temple!
STEVE: Good evening.
MAVIS: Did I hear you ordering a taxi?
TEMPLE: Yes.
MAVIS: Well, where are you going? Perhaps I can give you a lift?
TEMPLE: Do you know Weldon Court?
MAVIS: Yes, of course. It's just over the river. I'm going past there. I'll be delighted to drop you.
TEMPLE: Are you sure it's not out of your way?
MAVIS: Yes, of course.
TEMPLE: (*To the PORTER*) Porter, I shan't need the taxi.
PORTER: Very good, sir.
STEVE: Have you been dining here, Mrs Russell?
MAVIS: No, I've been addressing a literary society. I usually do that sort of thing about once a month – for my sins. (*Laughing*) It's been rather fun tonight. I was going great guns until some long haired genius asked me my opinion of Lawrence Durrell.

START FADE.

STEVE: Oh, dear!

168

MAVIS: I was brilliant – considering I've never read him.

STEVE: He'd probably never read him himself.

MAVIS: (*Laughing*) That's more than likely!

COMPLETE FADE.

FADE IN the sound of MAVIS RUSSELL's car: it is cruising along at an average speed.

TEMPLE and MAVIS are sitting in the front – MAVIS driving. STEVE is in the back of the car.

MAVIS: Do you think the police will ever find out who murdered Richard Ferguson?

TEMPLE: Yes, I do. But it isn't only a question of finding out who murdered him.

MAVIS: What do you mean?

TEMPLE: We want to know what's behind all this. We want to know why Max Wyman was murdered and why a gentleman called Jonathan sent Ferguson a mysterious postcard.

MAVIS: (*Faintly impatient*) If you ask me, the police attach far too much importance to this Jonathan person.

TEMPLE: (*A shrug*) Well, that's a point of view.

A tiny pause.

STEVE: When did you first hear about Richard Ferguson, Mrs Russell?

MAVIS: You mean – about the murder?

STEVE: Yes.

MAVIS: First thing this morning. Mark Elliot telephoned me.

STEVE: Were you surprised?

MAVIS: Yes, of course I was surprised!

TEMPLE: I thought that you were very fond of Richard Ferguson?

MAVIS: Yes, I was.

TEMPLE: Well, forgive me saying so, Mrs Russell, but – you don't seem unduly perturbed by the fact that he's been murdered.

MAVIS: I'm not easily perturbed, as you call it. I'm the unemotional type. It takes a great deal to upset me.

TEMPLE: Quite the opposite from Dinah, in fact.

MAVIS: What do you mean?

TEMPLE: She was so upset – when she heard about Richard – that she tried to commit suicide.

MAVIS: What! No, I don't believe it!

STEVE: It's true.

MAVIS: Is she all right?

TEMPLE: Yes, she will be.

MAVIS: Oh, the stupid girl! (*Pause*) I wish that car would get a move on or let me pass.

A pause.

MAVIS: Are you all right at the back, Mrs Temple?

STEVE: Yes, thanks.

MAVIS: I'm afraid there isn't a lot of room.

STEVE: That's all right. (*With a little laugh*) But I keep putting my feet on your hat box. I hope it won't mark.

MAVIS: My hat box?

STEVE: Yes.

MAVIS: Is there a hat box at the back?

STEVE: Yes. A small one: it's half under your seat.

MAVIS: But that's funny, I don't remember …

MAVIS slows down and turns slightly round in her seat.

TEMPLE: Wait a minute. (*He turns and leans over the back of his seat*) Where is it, Steve?

STEVE pulls out the case.

STEVE: There it is.

TEMPLE: (*To MAVIS*) It's a small brown case with a leather buckle.

MAVIS: (*Laughing*) Well, I don't know how it got there – it's not mine.

TEMPLE: Pull up!

MAVIS: But we're just going over the bridge; surely we can wait until we get across.

TEMPLE: (*Interrupting MAVIS: forcefully*) Do as I say – pull up!

TEMPLE snatches the handbrake. The car screeches to a standstill.

TEMPLE throws open the car door and jumps out: he opens the back door of the car.

STEVE: What are you going to do?

TEMPLE: (*Quickly*) Mind your feet, Steve – let me get the case!

MAVIS: What on earth …?

TEMPLE: (*Urgently*) Have you seen this case before?

MAVIS: No, I haven't! It doesn't look like a hat box!

TEMPLE: It doesn't <u>sound</u> like a hat box either!

STEVE: (*Alarmed*) Paul, what are you going to do?

TEMPLE: Stay where you are. I'm going to throw it into the river!

STEVE: Thank heavens Paul realised what it was.

A pause: followed by a distant splash and then a sudden detonation.

A pause.

TEMPLE: (*Seriously*) You're a very lucky woman, Mrs Russell. I don't have to tell you what would have happened if you hadn't given us a lift.

MAVIS: You mean that someone planted that thing in my car so that …

TEMPLE: Exactly.

MAVIS: (*Breathlessly*) Mr Temple, I … I just don't
            know what to say.

TEMPLE: Don't say anything, Mrs Russell. Move over.
            I'll drive.

The car door closes.

FADE UP of the car engine.

FADE SCENE.

*FADE UP of the car drawing to a standstill followed by the
sound of the car door opening and closing as TEMPLE and
STEVE alight.*

There is a faint background of street noises.

TEMPLE: Well, thank you for the lift.

MAVIS: Thank <u>you</u>.

TEMPLE: Are you all right? Do you think you can drive?

MAVIS: Yes, I'm perfectly all right. (*A little laugh*) I'm
            afraid I wasn't very cool, calm and collected on
            that occasion, was I?

STEVE: Have you any idea who planted that thing in the
            car?

MAVIS: (*A moment*) No, I haven't.

TEMPLE: Have you any idea <u>why</u> it was planted there?

MAVIS: (*Trying to be rather indifferent about it all*) I
            can't imagine. It wasn't exactly a friendly
            gesture, was it?

TEMPLE: That rather depends on your friends. Anyway,
            I'll report the incident to the Inspector – if
            anything else like that happens get in touch
            with me.

MAVIS: You can depend on that, Mr Temple! Goodbye!
            Thanks again.

TEMPLE: Goodbye.

The car drives away.

FADE the car.

FADE SCENE.

FADE UP of TEMPLE and STEVE entering Weldon Court.

STEVE: Let's walk up, Paul – don't wait for the lift.

TEMPLE: Yes, all right.

PORTER: Good evening, sir. Can I help you?

TEMPLE: No, thanks. We're just going up to Miss Nelson's flat.

PORTER: Number 3, sir …

TEMPLE: Yes, thank you.

PORTER: But I'm afraid Miss Nelson's out, sir.

TEMPLE: (*Surprised*) Out?

STEVE: Are you sure?

PORTER: Yes, madam. She went out about ten minutes ago.

TEMPLE: (*Puzzled*) About ten minutes ago?

PORTER: Yes, sir.

TEMPLE: Well, that's rather odd. She's expecting us.

PORTER: You can try the flat if you like, sir. (*Very dubious*) She might have come back, but I don't think so, sir.

TEMPLE: Well, we'll try the flat anyway. Come along, Steve.

FADE SCENE.

FADE UP of TEMPLE ringing the bell of DINAH's flat: we can hear the bell ringing inside the flat.
A slight pause.

STEVE: There's no one in.

TEMPLE: It doesn't look like it.

STEVE: I wonder what's happened, Paul?

TEMPLE: (*Thoughtfully*) I don't know.

STEVE: What did Mackintosh sound like on the telephone?

173

TEMPLE:	M'm – he sounded quite bright.
STEVE:	Do you think Dinah knew that he was phoning you?
TEMPLE:	No, I don't think she did.
STEVE:	Well, you can see what's happened! When he told her that he'd sent for you she obviously refused to … (*She stops suddenly*)
TEMPLE:	(*Quietly*) There is someone in the flat.
STEVE:	Yes … There's someone coming …

A long pause.

STEVE:	(*A whisper*) Hello, what's happening?
TEMPLE:	(*Quietly*) I don't know, but there's someone on the other side of the door.
CHARLES:	(*From inside the flat: in obvious pain: having dragged himself towards the door*) Who is it? Who's there?
TEMPLE:	This is Temple! Who is that?
CHARLES:	It's Rudolf Charles, I … I …
TEMPLE:	What is it? What's the matter?
CHARLES:	I've been shot, Temple, I …
TEMPLE:	Try to open the door!
CHARLES:	I can't, I …
TEMPLE:	Charles, listen. Try to open it.
CHARLES:	It's locked …The door's locked, Temple. I … I … can't … (*He is obviously in great pain*)
STEVE:	Paul, he sounds bad!
TEMPLE:	Get away from the door, Charles! Keep back!

TEMPLE starts to throw his weight against the door: the lock finally breaks.

STEVE:	You've done it, Paul.

The door is thrown open.

TEMPLE:	(*Quickly*) Now, what is it? What's happened?
STEVE:	Oh, Paul, look! He's bleeding badly. I'd better phone for a doctor!

CHARLES: I've been shot, I – I … Temple, listen … I've got to tell you something … it's very important …

TEMPLE: What is it, Charles?

CHARLES: Ferguson … is … the ring … (*He stops speaking*)

STEVE: (*A little frightened*) Paul!

A pause.

TEMPLE: (*Softly*) He's dead …

A long pause.

STEVE: What was it he said?

TEMPLE: He said: Ferguson … is … the … ring …

STEVE: (*Puzzled*) Ferguson is the ring? What on earth did he mean, Paul?

Dramatic FADE UP of music.

END OF EPISODE SIX

EPISODE SEVEN

AN INVITATION
FOR MR ELLIOT

OPEN TO:

TEMPLE: There's someone on the other side of the door.

CHARLES: (*From inside the flat: in obvious pain: having dragged himself towards the door*) Who is it? Who's there?

TEMPLE: This is Temple! Who is that?

CHARLES: It's Rudolf Charles, I … I …

TEMPLE: What is it? What's the matter?

CHARLES: I've been shot, Temple, I …

TEMPLE: Try to open the door!

CHARLES: I can't, I …

TEMPLE: Charles, listen. Try to open it.

CHARLES: It's locked … The door's locked, Temple. I … I … can't … (*He is obviously in great pain*)

STEVE: Paul, he sounds bad!

TEMPLE: Get away from the door, Charles! Keep back!

TEMPLE starts to throw his weight against the door: the lock finally breaks.

STEVE: You've done it, Paul.

The door is thrown open.

TEMPLE: (*Quickly*) Now, what is it? What's happened?

STEVE: Oh, Paul, look! He's bleeding badly. I'd better phone for a doctor!

CHARLES: I've been shot, I – I … Temple, listen … I've got to tell you something … it's very important …

TEMPLE: What is it, Charles?

CHARLES: Ferguson … is … the ring … (*He stops speaking*)

STEVE: (*A little frightened*) Paul!

A pause.

TEMPLE: (*Softly*) He's dead …

A long pause.

179

STEVE: What was it he said?

TEMPLE: He said: Ferguson … is … the … ring …

STEVE: (*Puzzled*) Ferguson is the ring? What on earth
            did he mean, Paul?

TEMPLE: I don't know. Look, Steve, go downstairs and
            get hold of the porter. Don't tell him what
            happened but ask him to come up here straight
            away.

STEVE: Yes, all right.

TEMPLE: While you're getting the porter I'll phone Sir
            Graham.

TEMPLE picks up the telephone and commences to dial.
FADE SCENE.

FADE UP the sound of the lift ascending; the lift gates open.

STEVE: (*Suddenly*) Oh, I was just coming down to see
            you. My husband would like to have a word
            with you – he's in Miss Nelson's flat.

PORTER: Was I wrong then, madam?

STEVE: Wrong?

PORTER: Is Miss Nelson in?

STEVE: No, she's out, but I think you'd better come and
            have a word with my husband.

PORTER: (*Curious*) Is anything the matter, madam?

STEVE: Mr Temple will tell you …

PORTER: (*Suddenly*) Oh, I forgot – there's a lady
            downstairs – in the hall – she's waiting for Mr
            Temple.

STEVE: Oh? Who is she – do you know?

PORTER: No, I'm sorry, I don't, madam. I've never seen
            her before.

STEVE: You go along to the flat. I'll see her.

STEVE enters the lift and closes the lift gates.
The lift descends.

180

The lift gates open.

STEVE: (*Surprised*) Why, Mrs Russell!

MAVIS: (*Rather tense*) Where's your husband, Mrs Temple? I must talk to him.

STEVE: Well, I'm afraid he's busy just now, but … What is it? Why did you come back? Did that business unnerve you? Are you frightened to drive?

MAVIS: No, it's not that, but … I changed my mind after what happened tonight. I think perhaps there are one or two things I ought to tell your husband …

STEVE: Such as?

MAVIS: Well – (*She hesitates*) – to begin with I lied about the ring. It wasn't sent to me: I wrote the note myself. You see, I'd had that ring for some time. Richard gave it to me.

STEVE: (*Surprised*) Richard gave it to you?

MAVIS: Yes.

STEVE: When?

MAVIS: About three months ago. I took him to London for a weekend: we stayed with some friends of mine in Chelsea. We did some shows, went to one or two parties, and – well – thoroughly enjoyed ourselves. Coming back in the car Richard suddenly kissed me and said that he wanted me to have the signet ring. I didn't want to take it, but I didn't want to hurt his feelings, so …

STEVE: So you took it.

MAVIS: Yes.

STEVE: Go on …

MAVIS: After the murder when everyone took it for granted that the dead man was Richard there

181

was a lot of talk about the missing ring. I nearly took it to the police and explained what had happened but …

STEVE: Why didn't you?

MAVIS: Well, everyone seemed to think that the ring had been taken by the murderer. I was already under suspicion. As you know, someone sent a magazine to Mr Ferguson with a message scrawled across it actually accusing me of the murder.

STEVE: You thought that if you produced the ring people would jump to the conclusion that you were implicated?

MAVIS: Exactly! And when your husband discovered that the dead man was not Richard, everybody said that obviously the person who had committed the murder had forgotten to complete the job by putting the ring on the dead man. So you see – which ever way you look at it – I was in a spot. Naturally I wanted to get rid of the ring, I wanted to hand it over to the police – but I didn't want to take any chances.

STEVE: So you pretended that it had been sent to you …

MAVIS: Yes. After I'd given it to your husband I went home. I hadn't been in the house a quarter of an hour when Richard phoned. He sounded worried and said he wanted the signet ring; that he must have it. I told him that I'd given it to your husband …

A long pause.

STEVE: I see.

MAVIS: That's the truth, Mrs Temple. I swear to you it's the truth. Don't you believe me?

182

A moment.

STEVE: Yes, I do, Mrs Russell – but I don't know if my husband will.

FADE UP of music.

FADE DOWN of music.
FADE IN the voice of SIR GRAHAM FORBES.

FORBES: … I still don't understand why Mackintosh telephoned you and asked you to go back to the flat.

TEMPLE: There are only two possible explanations, Sir Graham. Either Mackintosh was telling the truth and Dinah Nelson did, quite genuinely, want to talk to me or Mackintosh had persuaded Dinah to – well – try and pull the wool over my eyes.

FORBES: Yes, but how do you explain that when you got to the flat both Miss Nelson and Mackintosh were missing? And how does Rudolf Charles fit into the picture?

TEMPLE: I think Mackintosh must have left the flat after he phoned me. Probably Dinah sent him away – on some pretext or other – and while he was out Rudolf Charles turned up.

FORBES: M'm.

TEMPLE: I'm afraid we shan't really know what happened until you pick up Dinah Nelson or Reggie Mackintosh.

FORBES: What about this story of Mrs Russell's, Temple? What do you make of that?

TEMPLE: I think her story's probably true. After all she did give me the ring and Richard did telephone me shortly afterwards.

183

FORBES: Which seems to imply that young Ferguson
             must have telephoned her, as she says he did,
             and that she must have told him that you had
             the ring.

TEMPLE: Exactly.

FORBES: But why did young Ferguson ask you to take
             the ring to Mrs Gulliver? Why not pick it up
             from you himself?

TEMPLE: He knew that if he came to me personally there
             was a chance that I'd tip the police off and he'd
             be picked up.

There is a knock on the door and the door opens.

TEMPLE: In any case, I'm almost sure that … (*He stops*)

GERRARD: (*In the doorway*) Excuse me, Sir Graham!

FORBES: Oh, come in, Inspector!

TEMPLE: Any luck?

GERRARD: We've picked up Mackintosh – but we've had
             no luck with the girl. It's my opinion she's
             making for Town.

TEMPLE: Have you told the Yard?

GERRARD: Yes, they're on the look out for her. Oh, we'll
             pick her up all right, it's just a matter of time.

FORBES: Where did you find Mackintosh?

GERRARD: Well, I suppose 'find' is hardly the right word,
             sir. He simply turned up.

FORBES: What do you mean?

GERRARD: We were taking photographs of Miss Nelson's
             flat – Foster was going through the usual
             fingerprint routine – there was a ring at the bell
             and, well – there was Mr Mackintosh.

FORBES: Was he surprised to see you?

GERRARD: Very – he was even more surprised when I
             yanked him down here to the police station.

TEMPLE: Did you tell him about Rudolf Charles?

GERRARD: I didn't tell him anything, sir.

FORBES: How does he seem?

GERRARD: He seems very worried; he keeps asking for Mr Temple.

FORBES: Come along, Temple – let's go down and have a word with him.

TEMPLE: Did you find the revolver, Inspector?

GERRARD: No, we didn't. We've turned the place upside down but it's not in the flat.

COMPLETE FADE.

FADE UP of TEMPLE.

TEMPLE: Hello, Mackintosh! I thought we had an appointment about an hour ago – at Miss Nelson's?

REGGIE: (*Bewildered and rather annoyed*) Mr Temple, what does this mean? What on earth is going on?

TEMPLE: Supposing you tell me, Mackintosh?

REGGIE: What do you mean?

TEMPLE: Well, didn't you phone me? Didn't you tell me that Miss Nelson was very much better and that you'd finally persuaded her to talk to me?

REGGIE: But she did want to see you, Mr Temple. Look, I think perhaps I'd better tell you exactly what happened.

TEMPLE: Yes, I think perhaps you'd better.

REGGIE: After you and Mrs Temple left the flat with Rudolf Charles I had a pretty frank talk with Dinah. I told her that the best thing she could do was to tell you or Scotland Yard everything she knew about Richard Ferguson. Everything she knew about this so-called Mr Jonathan.

TEMPLE: How did she take it?

185

REGGIE:	Well, she began to get rather hysterical again and I thought I should have sent for a doctor. Anyway, I went into the kitchen and made a pot of tea. When I got back into the bedroom she seemed much brighter. She told me that she'd decided that the best thing she could do was to see Mr Temple again and make a clean breast of things. Naturally, I was very pleased about this, and telephoned you, Mr Temple.
FORBES:	Go on, Mackintosh.
REGGIE:	When I returned to the bedroom Dinah said that she'd got rather a bad headache and she asked me if I'd go to the chemist and get her some aspirin. Well, the first shop I called at was closed so I had to walk round the block and almost as far as the bridge. I suppose I was away from the flat about a quarter of an hour. When I got back the flat was empty. Dinah had disappeared.
FORBES:	The flat was empty?
REGGIE:	Yes.
FORBES:	Quite empty?
REGGIE:	Well, there was no one there!
TEMPLE:	Go on, Mackintosh.
REGGIE:	At first I just didn't know what to do. I knew that you would be coming at any moment and that, to say the least, you'd think it strange – after our phone conversation – to find the flat deserted. Suddenly, I got it into my head that Dinah might attempt to commit suicide again. I dashed downstairs and ran as far as the river; I thought – well I don't have to tell you what I was thinking. But there was no sign of Dinah. I walked into the town, made one or two calls,

	called in at The Encounter and then returned to the flat.
FORBES:	And you found Inspector Gerrard there?
REGGIE:	I did – much to my surprise! Mr Temple, tell me – has anything happened to Dinah?
TEMPLE:	So far as we know, nothing – beyond the fact that she's disappeared.
REGGIE:	Then why was the Inspector in the flat? They were taking photographs of the place and …
TEMPLE:	(*Interrupting REGGIE*) Mackintosh, when you returned to the flat – the first time, I mean – after getting the aspirin – you're quite sure it was empty?
REGGIE:	Yes, I've told you!
TEMPLE:	There was no sign of Rudolf Charles, for instance?
REGGIE:	Charles? Why, no!
FORBES:	Well, if you're telling the truth, Mackintosh, shortly after you left the flat for the second time Rudolf Charles turned up. He was there when Mr and Mrs Temple arrived.
REGGIE:	Rudolf was?
TEMPLE:	Yes, he'd been shot.
REGGIE:	Shot! I don't believe it! You're lying! You're just trying to trap me into …
FORBES:	Charles is dead.
REGGIE:	What!
FORBES:	He was shot – and it's my opinion, Mackintosh, that if you didn't shoot Charles yourself then Miss Nelson did.
TEMPLE:	So you <u>must</u> have seen the body of Rudolf Charles when you returned to the flat.

The door opens.

REGGIE: I tell you I didn't! If I'd seen him I would have
            ... (*He stops speaking*)
FORBES: What is it, Inspector?
GERRARD: They've found Dinah Nelson, sir.
TEMPLE: Where is she?
GERRARD: She's in hospital.
REGGIE: What's happened?
GERRARD: They pulled her out of the Thames about half
            an hour ago.
FORBES: So your guess was right, Mr Mackintosh.

FADE UP of music.

FADE DOWN of music.
A door opens and closes.
DOCTOR: Now do be careful, Mr Temple, please.
            Remember   Miss   Nelson's   extremely
            overwrought.
TEMPLE: Yes, doctor.
DOCTOR: I'll give you exactly. (*Glancing at his watch*)
            ... Five minutes.
TEMPLE: I shan't stay a second longer, I promise you.
DOCTOR: Quite frankly, Mr Temple, I'm not letting
            anyone else see her, in spite of what Sir
            Graham says.
TEMPLE: I understand, doctor.
The door opens.
DOCTOR: Now don't forget what I've told you.
The door closes.
DINAH: (*Softly; tensely*) Who is that?
TEMPLE: Hello, Dinah ...
DINAH: Who is it?
TEMPLE: (*Crossing to the bed*) It's Temple ...
DINAH: Oh ... Oh, Mr Temple ...
TEMPLE: How are you? How are you feeling, Dinah?

DINAH: I – I feel better than I did, I … (*Weakly*) Mr
            Temple, I'm sorry about this, I wouldn't have
            done it only …
TEMPLE: (*Quietly*) Now, Dinah, listen, I haven't much
            time; the doctor won't let me stay very long
            because they want you to rest. Now, what
            happened tonight, Dinah? Did you … shoot …
            Rudolf Charles?
DINAH: Yes … I did … Is he dead?
TEMPLE: Tell me what happened?
DINAH: He came to the flat … I'd sent Reggie out for
            some aspirin. Rudolf worked for Jonathan, you
            know. He was one of his right hand men, he …
            told … me … that … (*She hesitates*) Jonathan
            wanted me to work for him; now that Richard
            was dead … he wanted me to take his place …
            Rudolf said that if I didn't he would tell the
            police that I'd … thrown suspicion on to Mrs
            Russell.
TEMPLE: Did you throw suspicion on to Mrs Russell?
DINAH: Yes. I sent the magazine to Mr and Mrs
            Ferguson. You see, I – I was jealous of Mavis, I
            thought she was in love with Richard …
TEMPLE: But, Dinah, when you tried to commit suicide
            the first time you left a note for Jonathan.
DINAH: Yes, I know I did. You see, he had already tried
            to persuade me to join forces with him; the visit
            from Rudolf Charles was just …
TEMPLE: Just another attempt to make you change your
            mind?
DINAH: Yes.
TEMPLE: Dinah, tell me: why was Richard Ferguson so
            keen on getting hold of the signet ring?

189

DINAH:	When he gave the ring to Mavis Russell several months ago he didn't realise then that it was important. Jonathan told him that he must get the ring back. Richard told me about it and I promised to help him. That's why I was so surprised when you …
TEMPLE:	When I produced the ring?
DINAH:	Yes. After I saw you I sent a message to Richard, through Mrs Gulliver, telling him that you'd got the ring. That's why he phoned you.
TEMPLE:	Dinah, why did Mrs Ferguson tell me to get in touch with you? I thought that you'd never met.
DINAH:	I met her several days ago in London. I told her that I was the person who sent that magazine. She probably guessed that I knew a great deal about Richard. That's why she told you to get in touch with me.
TEMPLE:	(*Not convinced*) I see. Dinah, after you shot Charles, what exactly happened?
DINAH:	I – I went down to the river, I was desperate. I know that Jonathan would never leave me alone …
TEMPLE:	Did you see Mackintosh?
DINAH:	(*Tensely*) No, no, I didn't.
TEMPLE:	Dinah, I don't know what you remember or not but Mr Mackintosh telephoned me: he said that you were feeling better and that you wanted to talk.
DINAH:	Yes, I did feel better. I had a headache but apart from that I was all right until …
TEMPLE:	Until Charles turned up?
DINAH:	Yes.

A moment.

TEMPLE: (*Softly*) Dinah, you know what I'm going to ask
            you, don't you?

DINAH: Please don't, Mr Temple! Please … don't …

TEMPLE: Who is Jonathan?

DINAH: I don't know …

TEMPLE: You must know, Dinah, otherwise …

DINAH: (*Overwrought*) Mr Temple, please! Please
            don't ask me, I …

TEMPLE: Dinah, listen. I'm pretty sure I know who
            Jonathan is – so even if you tell me you're only
            confirming what I already know. (*A moment*)
            You don't believe me?

DINAH: No …

TEMPLE: (*Smiling*) You think I'm bluffing – don't you?

DINAH: Yes, I do.

TEMPLE: Well, I'll tell you what I'll do, Dinah. I'll strike
            a bargain with you. I'll tell you all I know
            about this business. I'll tell you why Richard
            Ferguson was murdered and who murdered
            him. I'll even tell you who Jonathan is.

DINAH: Well?

TEMPLE: If I'm right you need only to confirm it. If I'm
            wrong – well, I give you my word I'll never ask
            you another question about the Jonathan
            mystery. Is it a deal?

DINAH: (*A moment*) Yes, all right.

TEMPLE: You'll be perfectly honest with me?

DINAH: Yes. Yes, I promise.

TEMPLE: Right! Well, we'll start at the beginning.
            (*START FADE*) It's my opinion that Max
            Wyman was murdered by Richard Ferguson for
            the simple reason that young Ferguson …

COMPLETE FADE.

Slow FADE UP background noises of the hotel dining room.
FADE IN of a WAITER speaking.

WAITER: … Would you like some more coffee, madam?

STEVE: No, thank you. What about you, darling?

TEMPLE: No thanks, but you can bring some more butter, waiter.

WAITER: Very good, sir.

STEVE: You seem very bright this morning.

TEMPLE: I feel very bright.

STEVE: I can't imagine why.

TEMPLE: Well, as a matter of fact, Steve, I had rather an interesting little bet last night with Dinah Nelson. I won. I always feel rather pleased with myself when I win.

STEVE: Yes, well you won't continue to feel rather pleased with yourself if you put that elbow in the marmalade!

TEMPLE: Oh, lord! (*Suddenly*) Hello, here's Ferguson!

A moment.

ROBERT: Good morning, Mrs Temple.

STEVE: Good morning!

TEMPLE: Good morning, Ferguson!

ROBERT: Am I interrupting your breakfast?

TEMPLE: No. No, not at all. Sit down.

ROBERT: (*Sitting down; in rather a sober mood*) Helen and I are leaving for London in about an hour's time. I just thought I'd say goodbye.

TEMPLE: We're going back to Town ourselves this afternoon, so if there's anything I can do for you just give me a ring.

ROBERT: That's very kind of you, Temple, but as a matter of fact we've made up our minds to go home.

STEVE: You mean – back to the States?

192

ROBERT: Yeah, Yeah, we've talked it over – Helen and I
            – and we feel it's kind of pointless just hanging
            on like this. Whatever happens now can't
            change the real issue so far as we're concerned.
            Richard's gone and all the investigating, all the
            theories in the world won't bring him back.

STEVE: Yes, I understand. How's Mrs Ferguson this
            morning?

ROBERT: Oh, she's much better. We had a heart to heart
            talk last night, Mrs Temple. I think we
            straightened out a few things. I certainly hope
            so. Of course, Helen's always been a highly
            strung person.

TEMPLE: What exactly happened last night? Was Elliot
            telling the truth?

ROBERT: Oh, yes! Yes, he was. As a matter of fact
            there's a perfectly simple explanation. Shortly
            after she left me – to go shopping – Helen met
            a girl called Dinah Nelson. Well, it appears that
            Dinah was a friend of Richard's and …

TEMPLE: Did your wife know Miss Nelson?

ROBERT: Apparently she did, Mrs Temple, but it was a
            surprise to me. She met her in London two or
            three days ago. Anyway, she and Helen started
            talking about Richard. In fact, not to put too
            fine a point on it, she more or less confirmed
            my opinion of him. She said that Richard had
            been blackmailing Mark Elliot. He'd already
            had nearly two thousand pounds out of him.
            Naturally, Helen was terribly upset. She went
            straight to The Encounter and handed Mr Elliot
            a cheque for nineteen hundred pounds. I must
            say Elliot's been very good about the whole
            business.

193

TEMPLE:	What was Richard blackmailing Elliot about, do you know?
ROBERT:	Well, apparently he had some letters belonging to Elliot. I gather they were not exactly discreet – however, that's Mr Elliot's affair – not mine.
TEMPLE:	Have you seen the letters?
ROBERT:	Yes. After I picked up Helen last night we went round to Mrs Gulliver's and collected one or two things that belonged to Richard.
STEVE:	Was the house empty?
ROBERT:	No, there was a police officer there, but he gave us permission to bring away one or two odds and ends. We found Mr Elliot's letters at the bottom of an old deed box.
STEVE:	Have you still got them?
ROBERT:	No, as soon as we realised what they were we took them down to The Encounter and handed them over to Elliot.
TEMPLE:	And what about the cheque?
ROBERT:	Oh, he took that all right. I insisted.
STEVE:	Here's Mrs Ferguson!
ROBERT:	(*Turning; rising*) I was just saying goodbye to Mr and Mrs Temple, Helen.
HELEN:	(*Quietly*) The car's ready, Robert.
ROBERT:	O.K. What about the cases?
HELEN:	They're down: they're just putting them into the car.
ROBERT:	Well, goodbye, Mrs Temple.
STEVE:	Goodbye, Mr Ferguson.
TEMPLE:	When are you actually going back to the States?
HELEN:	We're flying back the day after tomorrow, Mr Temple.

TEMPLE: Well, look here, why don't you drop into the
             flat tomorrow for a drink? We shall be
             delighted to see you.
HELEN: Well, I'm afraid we have rather a busy day.
TEMPLE: (*Pleasantly*) Nonsense! You can always find
             time for a drink. Let's say twelve thirty.
ROBERT: (*Laughing*) O.K. Twelve thirty. It's a date. See
             you tomorrow.
HELEN: Well – au revoir, Mrs Temple.
STEVE: Au revoir, Mrs Ferguson.
A pause.
STEVE: (*Thoughtfully*) You know, I've just realised
             something …
TEMPLE: What's that?
STEVE: I don't know why, but – I don't like Mr
             Ferguson.
TEMPLE suddenly starts to laugh.
TEMPLE: By Timothy, women are extraordinary!
STEVE: What do you mean – women are extraordinary?
TEMPLE: Pass the toast.
STEVE: Now look here, Paul …
TEMPLE: Pass the toast, darling.
STEVE: Never mind the toast! What do you mean –
             women are extraordinary?
FORBES: (*Interrupting STEVE*) Good morning, Steve!
STEVE: Oh, hello, Sir Graham!
FORBES: You seem highly amused, Temple!
TEMPLE: I am, Sir Graham.
STEVE: He's laughing at one of his own remarks – and
             a very silly one too!
TEMPLE: I simply said women are extraordinary – and
             they are extraordinary, aren't they, Sir
             Graham?

FORBES:	Don't try and drag me into this! I'm strictly neutral.
TEMPLE:	Sit down and have some coffee.
FORBES:	No thanks. Steve, I want you to take a good look at these photographs.
STEVE:	What are they, Sir Graham?
FORBES:	Have you seen this man before?
STEVE:	Why yes! Paul, look!
TEMPLE:	Why, he's the fellow who impersonated Max Wyman! He was clean shaven when we saw him, but that's the man all right!
FORBES:	Are you sure?
TEMPLE:	Positive.
FORBES:	Good! Now what about this gentleman?
A moment.	
STEVE:	(*Thoughtfully*) No, I don't recognise him …
TEMPLE:	Wait a minute, Steve! Isn't he the character that let us into Mrs Gulliver's? He was using the vacuum cleaner and said he worked for a domestic help service of some sort.
STEVE:	Yes! Yes, I think you're right, darling!
FORBES:	You're sure, Temple?
TEMPLE:	Yes, I'm pretty sure.
FORBES:	Good! We picked them up this morning.
TEMPLE:	(*Surprised*) Both of them?
FORBES:	Both of them. (*Amused*) Oh, we can move fast, Temple, when we want to.
TEMPLE:	(*Laughing*) I know that, Sir Graham. What happened?
FORBES:	I haven't got the details. Gerrard phoned me about an hour ago. They picked them up in an amusement arcade just off the Tottenham Court Road.
STEVE:	Were they together?

FORBES:	Yes.
TEMPLE:	Who are they, Sir Graham?
FORBES:	Well, this fellow – the one who impersonated Wyman – used to be in the confidence racket. His name's James – Ed James. He's a first class driver: did pretty well in one of the Monte Carlo rallies.
TEMPLE:	Really? And the other fellow?
FORBES:	Oh, that's Clegley, a very different type. He's really vicious. We've been wanting to pin something on that gentleman for a very long time. Incidentally, he was a friend of Red Harris's.
TEMPLE:	Clegley was?
FORBES:	Yes.
STEVE:	Sir Graham, do you think Red Harris, Ed James and this man Clegley actually worked for Jonathan?
FORBES:	Yes. Jonathan has a pretty big hold on the car racket. It's my opinion that men like James and Clegley actually steal the cars and men like Red Harris fence them.
STEVE:	Then why did they get rid of Red Harris? He must have been a pretty important part of the set up.
TEMPLE:	I should imagine that someone told Jonathan that I'd been in touch with Red.
FORBES:	Yes. They probably knew that Red owed you a favour, Temple, and they weren't taking any chances.
STEVE:	Well, how did young Ferguson fit into the picture?
FORBES:	I think Richard Ferguson must have acted as a sort of liaison for Jonathan: in other words it

197

	was his job to make certain that the cars which were stolen were actually passed over to the organisation and not sold independently.
STEVE:	I suppose that explains the card he received.
TEMPLE:	Yes, the card gave him the two numbers – the genuine number and the number he had to change over to. In other words … (*He notices the PORTER*) Yes, what is it?
PORTER:	Excuse me, sir.
TEMPLE:	Yes?
PORTER:	There's a gentleman to see you, sir! A Mr Elliot.
TEMPLE:	Mr Elliot?
PORTER:	Yes, sir. He's waiting for you in the lounge, sir.
TEMPLE:	Oh, thank you.
PORTER:	Thank you, sir.
TEMPLE:	Now what does Elliot want, I wonder? I'll see you upstairs, darling.
STEVE:	Yes, all right, Paul.
TEMPLE:	Are you packed?
STEVE:	I shall be by the time you're ready. Goodbye, Sir Graham.
FORBES:	Goodbye, Steve. What time are you leaving, Temple?
TEMPLE:	Oh, not till this afternoon, Sir Graham. I should imagine we'll get off about three.
FORBES:	Splendid. You can give me a lift.
TEMPLE:	Shall we pick you up at the police station or …
FORBES:	No. No, I'll be here, Temple.
TEMPLE:	Oh, Sir Graham – did you – er – speak to them at the hospital about …?
FORBES:	Yes, I did. I'm afraid it wasn't easy.
TEMPLE:	I didn't think it would be.
FORBES:	Still, don't worry. It's fixed.

TEMPLE: Good.
FADE SCENE.

FADE IN of TEMPLE:
TEMPLE: Hello, Elliot! Sorry to have kept you waiting.
MARK: (*Nervously*) That's all right, Temple. I hope I
            haven't interrupted your breakfast.
TEMPLE: No, we've just finished. You're nice and early
            this morning.
MARK: Yes; I'm just on my way to London. I've got an
            early luncheon appointment.
TEMPLE: Well – what can I do for you?
MARK: Temple, you remember I told you about
            Richard Ferguson blackmailing me and – about
            – the – letters – I wrote?
TEMPLE: Yes, I remember …
MARK: Well, look here, Temple. If you catch the
            person that murdered Richard Ferguson, does
            that mean I shall have to get up in court and tell
            the whole story?
TEMPLE: You mean about Ferguson blackmailing you?
MARK: Yes.
TEMPLE: Well, it depends entirely on who murdered
            Ferguson and what the motive was. You may
            not have to get up in court at all.
MARK: (*Not too sure*) I see.
TEMPLE: I don't think you do see. At least, if you do,
            you don't look very happy about it.
MARK: (*A note of tenseness creeping into his voice*)
            Temple, if anyone claims – in court or
            anywhere else – that I had a motive for
            murdering Richard Ferguson I shall deny it. In
            spite of what I've already told you – I shall
            deny it!

199

TEMPLE:	(*Quietly*) So Ferguson was telling the truth.
MARK:	What do you mean?
TEMPLE:	You've got the letters back, haven't you, Elliot?
MARK:	Yes.
TEMPLE:	(*Lightly*) Well, if you've got them back, so far as I can see, there's nothing for you to worry about.
MARK:	Unless …
TEMPLE:	Unless what?
MARK:	Unless the police fail to find the person who murdered Ferguson and pick on me as a sort of scapegoat.
TEMPLE:	If the police don't think you murdered Ferguson they won't pick on you. I've got a shrewd suspicion that the police already know who murdered Ferguson. (*Suddenly*) Elliot, I'm afraid you'll have to excuse me, I've got rather a lot to do and I'm going back to Town myself this afternoon.
MARK:	Yes, of course. Oh, by the way, I was awfully sorry to hear about Dinah Nelson.
TEMPLE:	Yes, it was a nasty business. I very much doubt if she'll get over it …
MARK:	(*Surprised*) Get over it? Haven't you heard?
TEMPLE:	What do you mean?
MARK:	Dinah Nelson's dead …
TEMPLE:	What?!
MARK:	I telephoned the hospital about half an hour ago. She died this morning.
TEMPLE:	Oh, I'm sorry about that. Sir Graham will be sorry too – he intended to have a talk with her this morning.
MARK:	Did anyone see her last night?

TEMPLE: No, it was quite out of the question. She was unconscious. Well, I'd better be making a move. (*Suddenly*) Oh, by the way, Elliot – how long are you going to be in Town?

MARK: Two or three nights.

TEMPLE: Well, I'd like to see you again. Drop in the flat sometime – you'll find my address in the book.

MARK: Well – thanks very much.

TEMPLE: (*Casually*) As a matter of fact we're having a few friends in tomorrow – about midday – just for a drink. Drop in then if you like.

MARK: I'd like to.

TEMPLE: Fine! Well – see you tomorrow. Goodbye.

MARK: (*Smiling*) Goodbye.

FADE IN of music.

FADE DOWN of music.

FADE IN of TEMPLE shaking a cocktail shaker.

STEVE: That's enough, Paul! You're shaking the ice all over the place.

TEMPLE stops shaking the cocktail.

TEMPLE: (*Unscrewing the shaker*) Give me your glass, Mrs Ferguson.

HELEN: Not for me, thanks! Two's my limit.

TEMPLE: Nonsense! (*Pouring out a drink; raising his voice*) Charlie!

CHARLIE: Yes, sir?

TEMPLE: We want another bottle of gin.

CHARLIE: Very good, sir.

STEVE: You'll find one in the kitchen, Charlie.

CHARLIE: Okedoke, Mrs Temple!

TEMPLE: Ferguson?

ROBERT: Well – just a spot, I guess.

TEMPLE pours out the drink.

TEMPLE: Steve?
STEVE: Thank you, darling.
TEMPLE pours out drinks.
A pause.
TEMPLE: (*Raising his glass*) Cheers!
ROBERT: Down the hatch!
A slight pause.
STEVE: I hope you have a pleasant trip back to the States, Mrs Ferguson.
HELEN: Thank you, Mrs Temple. Thank goodness the weather looks quite promising.
STEVE: Are you staying over in New York for a few days?
HELEN: No, we're going on to Detroit as soon as possible.
ROBERT: Which reminds me, Helen! I ought to have checked on the trains from New York. I'll ring the tourist people when I get back to the hotel.
HELEN: Mr Temple … (*Hesitantly*) There's something I wanted to say before we go.
ROBERT: (*With quiet sincerity*) There's something we both want to say. Temple, I lost my temper the other day when Sir Graham was questioning us, but – well …
HELEN: We don't want you to think that we're not grateful.
TEMPLE: Grateful for what?
ROBERT: You've worked very hard on this case, Temple, and we'd like you to know that just because you haven't got any results it doesn't mean to say that …
TEMPLE: (*Interrupting ROBERT*) Now wait a minute! What sort of results were you expecting?

202

HELEN: Well – we were hoping that you'd find out who murdered Richard.

TEMPLE: (*Smiling*) But I know who murdered Richard.

HELEN: (*Astounded*) What!

ROBERT: Say – are you serious?

TEMPLE: I also know why Richard wanted the signet ring, why the body of Max Wyman was found in your son's flat and I also know the identity of Jonathan …

ROBERT: What!

HELEN: You know who Jonathan is?

The flat buzzer is ringing: during the following dialogue CHARLIE answers the door.

ROBERT: Temple, is this a joke?!

TEMPLE: It's no joke, Ferguson. As a matter of fact I've invited Jonathan here – to the flat – this morning.

ROBERT: You don't really mean that!

The door opens.

CHARLIE: Excuse me, sir …

TEMPLE: Yes – what is it, Charlie?

CHARLIE: (*Quite chirpily*) A Mr Mackintosh to see you, sir.

Dramatic FADE UP of music.

END OF EPISODE SEVEN

EPISODE EIGHT

JONATHAN

OPEN TO:

TEMPLE: I also know why Richard wanted the signet ring, why the body of Max Wyman was found in your son's flat and I also know the identity of Jonathan …

ROBERT: What!

HELEN: You know who Jonathan is?

The flat buzzer is ringing: during the following dialogue CHARLIE answers the door.

ROBERT: Temple, is this a joke?!

TEMPLE: It's no joke, Ferguson. As a matter of fact I've invited Jonathan here – to the flat – this morning.

ROBERT: You don't really mean that!

The door opens.

CHARLIE: Excuse me, sir …

TEMPLE: Yes – what is it, Charlie?

CHARLIE: (*Quite chirpily*) A Mr Mackintosh to see you, sir.

TEMPLE: Ah, come in, Mackintosh! Come in!

REGGIE: (*Entering*) I got your note this morning, Mr Temple, so I thought …

TEMPLE: (*Interrupting REGGIE*) Delighted to see you, my dear fellow! (*Dismissing CHARLIE*) Don't forget the gin!

CHARLIE: Very good, sir!

REGGIE: Good morning, Mrs Temple!

STEVE: Good morning, Mr Mackintosh!

ROBERT: Look, Temple, I don't want to be rude but I think you owe us an explanation.

TEMPLE: An explanation?

ROBERT: Yes. Just before Mackintosh arrived you made a startling statement. You said …

207

TEMPLE:	(*Interrupting ROBERT: brightly*) Oh, I'm sorry, Mackintosh! Do you know Mr and Mrs Ferguson?
REGGIE:	(*Faintly surprised*) Why, no! I don't think we've met.
HELEN:	(*Tensely*) Mr Temple, please! Do you really know who murdered Richard?
TEMPLE:	Yes, Charlie?
CHARLIE:	Mr Elliot, sir!
TEMPLE:	Ah, come in, Elliot!
MARK:	(*Entering; pleasantly*) Good morning, Temple! Sorry I'm a little late. (*Surprised*) Why, hello, Ferguson! Good morning, Mrs Ferguson.
HELEN:	Good morning!
TEMPLE:	I think you've met Mr Mackintosh?
MARK:	Yes, of course. I was sorry to hear about your sister-in-law, Mackintosh.
ROBERT:	(*Aggressively; making himself heard*) Look, Temple, I don't want to be rude but …
TEMPLE:	You've said that before, Ferguson!

An embarrassing silence.

MARK:	Is – er – anything the matter?
REGGIE:	Have we interrupted something, Mr Temple?
ROBERT:	(*Calmly*) Just before you arrived Temple made an extraordinary statement. My wife and I want an explanation.
HELEN:	We most certainly do!
REGGIE:	(*Puzzled*) What did you say, Mr Temple?
MARK:	(*Smiling*) Yes, what was this shattering statement of yours?
TEMPLE:	(*Quietly*) Tell them, Ferguson.
ROBERT:	He said he knew who murdered Richard.
REGGIE:	What!?

ROBERT: Not only that but he said that he knew the identity of Jonathan and that he was actually coming here – to the flat – this morning.

MARK: (*Surprised*) Did you say that?

REGGIE: Is it true, Mr Temple?

TEMPLE: (*After a moment*) Well, sit down, Elliot – Mackintosh. (*A slight pause*) Well, I think the best thing I can do is begin at the beginning. This isn't going to be very pleasant, Ferguson, as far as you and your wife are concerned, but ...

ROBERT: That's all right, Temple. Don't spare our feelings. You go ahead.

TEMPLE: Well, for a very long time now there's been a set up in this country, dealing in stolen cars. The set up was controlled by a person called Jonathan. Richard Ferguson worked for him but one day, for reasons which we won't go into at the moment, Richard suddenly decided that he wanted to drop the whole business. He knew it was no good talking to Jonathan ...

MARK: You mean, he decided to eliminate Max Wyman and give Jonathan and everyone else the impression that he – Ferguson – had been murdered?

TEMPLE: Exactly! He'd always hated Max Wyman because Wyman mistrusted him. He knew that there was a resemblance between Wyman and himself. People had in fact frequently mistaken them for each other, so he felt pretty sure that he'd get away with it providing he disfigured Wyman, dressed him up in his clothes, and faked the fingerprints. He invited Wyman to his

	flat and – well – you know what happened. Unfortunately, however, young Ferguson …
REGGIE:	Forgot the signet ring …
TEMPLE:	What do you mean, Mackintosh, forgot the signet ring?
REGGIE:	He forgot to put his ring on the dead man – that's true, isn't it?
TEMPLE:	No. I'm afraid it isn't.
REGGIE:	(*Surprised*) No?
TEMPLE:	No, Ferguson hadn't got the ring – he'd given it to Mrs Russell. (*Smiling*) But quite a lot of people thought the same as you, Mackintosh, including Red Harris. Except that Red thought that Jonathan actually helped young Ferguson to murder Wyman and that they had both forgotten the ring.
ROBERT:	(*Faintly irritated*) Yes, this is all very interesting, Temple, but you said that you knew the identity of Jonathan.
TEMPLE:	I do. As a matter of fact he's here – now – in this very room.
ROBERT:	Jonathan?
TEMPLE:	Yes.
MARK:	(*Astounded*) What!?
ROBERT:	But he can't be here unless …
REGGIE:	(*Tensely*) What are you looking at me like that for?
TEMPLE:	(*Slowly*) Don't you know why, Mackintosh?
REGGIE:	Temple, you surely don't think I'm – Jonathan?
TEMPLE:	Aren't you?
REGGIE:	You're mad. Completely mad.
STEVE:	Paul, look out!
REGGIE:	(*Tensely*) Stand back! Stand back, everybody!

TEMPLE: Put that gun down, Mackintosh! Do you hear me? Put it down!

REGGIE: I warn you, Temple! One step more and by God I'll …

STEVE: Paul, don't!

A moment.

REGGIE: That's better! Now stand over there near Ferguson …

CHARLIE enters.

CHARLIE: (*Quite chirpily*) Sorry to 'ave been so long, Mr Temple, I 'ad a bit of a job finding the gin and …

REGGIE: Drop that bottle!

CHARLIE: (*Amazed*) Hello, what's going on 'ere?!

REGGIE: You heard what I said! Drop that bottle!

STEVE: Drop it, Charlie!

CHARLIE drops the bottle.

REGGIE: Now stand over there next to Mrs Temple. (*A moment*) You heard me …

TEMPLE: Do as he tells you, Charlie.

REGGIE: Go on – get moving …

CHARLIE: (*Watching REGGIE: surly*) O.K.

CHARLIE moves across the room.

REGGIE: Now listen – I warn you – if anybody moves – if anybody tries any tricks – you've had it!

HELEN: (*Tensely*) Don't anyone move. He means it.

REGGIE: Have you got the key to this door, Temple?

TEMPLE: It's in the lock on the outside.

REGGIE: Open the door, Mrs Temple.

A slight pause.

TEMPLE: Open it, Steve.

The door opens.

REGGIE: Now go back into the room, Mrs Temple.

TEMPLE: (*From the background*) You fool, Mackintosh! You don't think you're going to get away with this, do you?

REGGIE: We'll see, Temple! We'll see!

The door opens and closes very quickly: we hear the sound of the key in the lock and the door being locked.

FADE in of TEMPLE, MARK ELLIOT, FERGUSON, STEVE and CHARLIE at the door: MARK is shaking the door handle: trying to force it.

CHARLIE: He's locked it, Mr Temple!

ROBERT: (*Tensely*) Temple, what are we going to do?

HELEN: Phone for the police!

MARK: We'd better break the lock, Temple, otherwise he'll have a good start on us!

TEMPLE: (*Calming them down*) Now, wait a minute!

MARK stops attacking the door.

TEMPLE: He won't have a start on anybody! Sir Graham's downstairs with Inspector Gerrard and half Scotland Yard. If he gets as far as the hall he'll be lucky!

STEVE: (*Suddenly*) Paul listen.

In the background: actually from the staircase we hear the sound of excited voices. MACKINTOSH is struggling: we can hear his voice shouting.

REGGIE: Leave me alone! Leave me alone! I warn you, I shall fire!

There is a sudden sound of a revolver shot.

Silence.

HELEN: Can't we get out and see what's happened?

We hear the sound of footsteps approaching the flat.

TEMPLE: Quiet! There's someone coming …

We hear the sound of a key in the lock.

TEMPLE: (*Calling*) Who's there?

The door opens.

STEVE: (*Relieved*) Oh, Sir Graham!
ROBERT: (*Quickly*) Did you get him?
MARK: What happened?
TEMPLE: What happened, Sir Graham?
FORBES: He's dead.
TEMPLE: Mackintosh?
FORBES: (*Nodding*) Yes. He shot himself.
Dramatic FADE UP of music.

FADE DOWN of music.
FADE IN the ringing of a telephone: the buzz-buzz signifying that the number is ringing out.
OPERATOR: Hello.
STEVE: Can I speak to Mr Mark Elliot, please?
OPERATOR: Who is it calling?
STEVE: Mrs Temple …
OPERATOR: One moment, please …
The OPERATOR rings the extension.
MARK: Hello?
OPERATOR: Mrs Temple on the line, sir.
MARK: Oh! Oh, thank you.
STEVE: Hello?
MARK: (*Surprised*) Good morning, Mrs Temple!
STEVE: (*With great charm*) Oh, good morning, Mr Elliot! I'm sorry if I've disturbed you.
MARK: Not at all. I've been up for hours. I've been reading the papers. There doesn't appear to be anything about Mackintosh.
STEVE: No, there doesn't.
MARK: Well, I'm glad for the Fergusons' sake.
STEVE: Mr Elliot, I rather wanted to talk to you, do you think we could meet some time today? I know you're a frightfully busy man.

213

MARK: Well, I've an appointment at five o'clock but – Look, let's say three-thirty.

STEVE: (*With almost girlish charm*) Three-thirty would do beautifully. Perhaps we could have tea together?

MARK: Yes, I – er – I don't see why not.

STEVE: I'll see you at the Ritz – in the hall – about three-thirty.

MARK: Yes, all right, Mrs Temple.

STEVE: It's very sweet of you.

MARK: Not at all. Delighted. (*Suddenly, pleasant yet curious*) Oh, by the way, what is it you wanted to see me about, Mrs Temple?

STEVE: (*With a tantalising little laugh*) I'll tell you this afternoon, Mr Elliot. Goodbye!

STEVE replaces the receiver.

TEMPLE: (*Delighted: but very keyed up*) Well done, Steve! Perfect!

STEVE: Next week 'Cleopatra'.

TEMPLE: What did he say?

STEVE: I'm having tea with him this afternoon. But don't ask me why!

The flat buzzer sounds in the background.

TEMPLE: (*Laughing*) I'll brief you later, Steve. Don't worry!

STEVE: What do you mean – 'brief' me? What's got into you this morning, Paul! You were up half the night and yet you seem … Yes, what is it, Charlie?

CHARLIE: Sir Graham Forbes is here, madam.

TEMPLE: Come in, Sir Graham! Come in!

FORBES: (*Entering: in a serious manner*) Hello, Temple! Good morning, Steve!

STEVE: Good morning, Sir Graham!

TEMPLE: (*Direct and to the point*) Well?
FORBES: I think you're going to be wrong, Temple.
TEMPLE: I don't think so.
FORBES: Well, it's beginning to look like it. Frankly, I'm
              worried. Did you telephone Mrs Russell?
TEMPLE: I saw her.
FORBES: (*Surprised*) You saw her? When?
TEMPLE: Last night. After the Mackintosh incident.
STEVE: Paul went back to Oxford, Sir Graham. He
              didn't get home till half-past four this morning.

The telephone rings.

FORBES: What did she say?
TEMPLE: I put my cards on the table and told her quite …
              Excuse me.

TEMPLE lifts the receiver.

TEMPLE: Hello?
MAVIS: (*On the other end of the line*) Mr Temple?
TEMPLE: Oh, hello, Mrs Russell!
MAVIS: I did what you suggested.
TEMPLE: Well?
MAVIS: He's made an appointment. Five o'clock this
              afternoon …
TEMPLE: Good. Did he say anything else?
MAVIS: No; he was non-committal, but I think he was
              interested …
TEMPLE: Thank you, Mrs Russell.
MAVIS: (*A shade nervous*) You – er – don't really want
              me to keep that appointment, do you?
TEMPLE: No. We'll keep it for you. Thanks very much,
              Mrs Russell.
MAVIS: I'm going away for two or three weeks. If – if
              you want to get in touch with me …
TEMPLE: (*Smiling*) Don't worry. If we want you we'll
              find you.

MAVIS: Goodbye, Mr Temple – and thanks for everything.
TEMPLE: Goodbye!
TEMPLE replaces the receiver.
FORBES: (*Eagerly*) Well?
TEMPLE: He made an appointment to see her this afternoon at five o'clock.
STEVE: (*Suddenly*) Mr Elliot said he had an appointment at five, Paul.
FORBES: How do you know, Steve?
TEMPLE: She spoke to Elliot on the phone, Sir Graham. As a matter of fact she's having tea with him this afternoon.
FORBES: Oh, is she!
TEMPLE: (*Suddenly, very serious*) Now listen, Steve! When you see Elliot this afternoon this is what I want you to do.
FADE SCENE.

FADE IN of music: a small piece orchestra playing light music.
FADE the music to the background.
FADE IN of STEVE talking: she is chatty and rather artificial: obviously, deliberately, boring MARK ELLIOT.
STEVE: … Of course if you do stick to one colour it's far more economical. I remember one year I wore nothing but grey. By the end of the season I was positively dying for something gay and exotic.
MARK: Yes, I'm – er – sure you were. (*Quickly, trying to change the subject*) Are you sure you wouldn't like another cake, Mrs Temple?
STEVE: Oh, quite sure, thank you.
MARK: Another cup of tea?

STEVE: No, thank you.

MARK: (*Suddenly*) Good gracious, it's four o'clock already.

STEVE: Is it really? Goodness, I have been talking, haven't I? And all about clothes, too! I'm sure you've been bored to tears, Mr Elliot.

MARK: No, of course not, but – er – Mrs Temple, what exactly is it you wanted to see me about?

STEVE: Oh, yes! Yes, of course! How stupid of me! Do you know, I'd almost forgotten. My husband asked me to give you a message, Mr Elliot. He couldn't come himself as he had an appointment at half-past three and another at five o'clock so it was quite … Oh, by the way, you've got an appointment at five, haven't you?

MARK: Yes, I have.

STEVE: Well, I hope I'm not going to make you late for it because …

MARK: No, no, no, there's plenty of time. It's only just four. (*Trying to be pleasant, controlling his impatience*) Mrs Temple, you still haven't told me?

STEVE: Told you what?

MARK: What you wanted to see me about?

STEVE: Oh, but I did! Just now. My husband asked me to deliver a message.

MARK: Yes, but – what was the message?

STEVE: Oh, of course! (*Quite brightly*) He said, tell Mr Elliot – the game's up.

MARK: The game's up?

STEVE: Yes.

MARK: What does he mean?

217

STEVE: (*Quite brightly*) I'm afraid I don't know, Mr Elliot. That's just the message I was asked to deliver.

MARK: Did your husband say anything else?

STEVE: No. Except that he insisted that I had tea with you down here instead of in your room. (*Suddenly*) Oh, that was only because he knew that there'll be a telephone in your room and he didn't want you to use it.

MARK: (*Puzzled*) He didn't want me to use it?

STEVE: Yes.

MARK: I'm sorry, but I'm afraid I just don't understand.

STEVE: Well, you see – Paul thought that once you saw our friend you might want to telephone someone and – well – that's the last thing he wanted you to do.

MARK: Our friend? Who are you talking about?

STEVE: Why, our friend over there, of course – in the corner …

MARK: I don't see anyone …

STEVE: Oh, come! Look carefully, Mr Elliot! In the corner – near the pillar.

MARK: (*Suddenly; staggered; dropping his cup on to the saucer*) Good lord! It's Mackintosh!!!

STEVE: Yes.

MARK: It's Mackintosh!

STEVE: (*Significantly*) Yes …

MARK: But – but I thought he was dead!

STEVE: Whatever gave you that idea?

MARK: But he shot himself! I heard the shot.

STEVE: We all heard the shot. But he couldn't very well shoot himself with a blank cartridge, now could he?

218

MARK: You mean the whole thing was a put up job? (*Slowly*) How much does your husband know, Mrs Temple?

STEVE: Quite a lot, I should imagine. Of course he doesn't tell me everything – you know what husbands are!

MARK: (*Angrily; leaning towards STEVE*) Now you listen to me, Mrs Temple …

STEVE: Let go of my arm!

MARK: You'll tell me exactly what's behind all this! You'll tell me why you came here this afternoon and why …

GERRARD: (*Interrupting MARK with authority*) Excuse me, sir! Mr Elliot?

MARK: (*Turning angry*) Yes? What do you want?

GERRARD: I'm Inspector Gerrard, sir, and this is Sergeant Bowman.

MARK: Well?

GERRARD: We have a warrant for your arrest, Mr Elliot.

MARK: My – my arrest?

GERRARD: Yes, sir.

STEVE: It looks as if you'll be wearing grey this season, Mr Elliot.

FADE UP of music.

FADE DOWN of music.
FADE IN background noises of the main hall of a large hotel.

FORBES: Good afternoon.

CLERK: Good afternoon, sir.

FORBES: I believe you have a Mr and Mrs Ferguson staying here?

CLERK: Yes, sir, Suite 103 …

FORBES: Well, would you ring Mr Ferguson please and say that – Mrs Russell has arrived?

219

CLERK:	Mrs Russell?
FORBES:	Yes.
CLERK:	(*Hesitating*) But – er …
FORBES:	(*Quietly, with authority*) My name is Forbes, Sir Graham Forbes of Scotland Yard. This gentleman is Paul Temple. Inspector Gerrard … Sergeant Wilson.
CLERK:	Oh! Oh, I see. I – er – think perhaps you'd better see Mr Milson, the manager, sir, just in case …
FORBES:	(*With authority*) Just ring Mr Ferguson and tell him that Mrs Russell has arrived. That's all we want you to do.
CLERK:	Very good, sir.

The CLERK lifts the telephone receiver.

CLERK:	Suite 103, please.

A moment.

We hear the operator clicking the room number.

A long pause.

FORBES:	Well?
CLERK:	There doesn't appear to be a reply, sir.
FORBES:	Keep ringing.
CLERK:	Yes, sir.

A pause.

We can hear the operator still clicking the number.

CLERK:	There's no reply, sir. I'm sorry.

The CLERK replaces the receiver.

MILSON:	(*Arriving on the scene*) What is it, Desmond?
CLERK:	These gentlemen are asking for Mr Ferguson, sir.
MILSON:	The Fergusons checked out about an hour ago.
TEMPLE:	(*Surprised*) Checked out?
MILSON:	Yes.
TEMPLE:	Did they take their luggage?

MILSON: (*Amused*) Yes, of course! They're leaving on the six o'clock plane for New York.

FADE UP of music.

FADE DOWN of music.
FADE UP noise and conversation of the departure hall at London Airport.
FADE the noise down gradually to the distant background.

ROBERT: (*Quietly; yet determined manner*) Are you o.k., Helen?

HELEN: (*Tensely*) Yes.

ROBERT: Now remember what I told you?

HELEN: I shall be all right when we get on the plane.

ROBERT: Sure.

A moment.

OFFICER: May I see your passports, please?

ROBERT: Certainly.

A tiny pause.

OFFICER: Have you any English money on you, Mr Ferguson?

ROBERT: Maybe a shilling or two.

OFFICER: Mrs Ferguson?

HELEN: No – no, nothing.

OFFICER: Thank you, sir.

ROBERT: Thank you!

2nd OFFICER:(*Approaching*) Oh, one moment, Mr Ferguson, please!

ROBERT: Yeah? What is it?

2nd OFFICER:Would you come this way, please, sir – the Immigration Officer would like to have a word with you?

ROBERT: (*After a momentary hesitation: pleasantly*) Surely, I won't be a moment, Helen.

HELEN: All right, Robert.

221

A pause.

GERRARD: Good evening, Mrs Ferguson!

HELEN: Oh! Oh, good evening, Inspector!

GERRARD: (*Gently*) Now you know why we're here, Mrs Ferguson, there's no need to attract attention to yourself.

HELEN: What do you mean?

GERRARD: I think you know what I mean. All right, sergeant!

HELEN: Let go! How dare you!

GERRARD: Now be sensible, Mrs Ferguson! Remember we can be just as noisy as you if we want to be – and twice as unpleasant!

HELEN: I'm – I'm sorry. What do you want me to do?

GERRARD: That's better. All right, sergeant – wait in the hall.

Slow FADE DOWN of background noises and conversation.

FADE UP of a door opening.

2nd OFFICER: This way, please, sir.

ROBERT: Thank you. (*Suddenly; apparently pleasantly surprised*) Why hello, Temple! Sir Graham!

FORBES: Thank you, sir.

The door closes.

ROBERT: (*Jovial manner*) This is a surprise! I certainly didn't expect to find you two at the airport!

TEMPLE: Well, if it comes to that we didn't expect to find you here either. You cancelled your hotel reservations this morning.

ROBERT: That's right, I did.

TEMPLE: But we thought you intended to stay over here for a couple of days?

ROBERT: So we did, but – say, you boys are pretty well informed!

222

FORBES:	(*Quietly*) What happened, Ferguson?
ROBERT:	Helen suddenly changed her mind <u>again</u> and decided that she wanted to go home at once. (*Laughing*) You know what women are!
TEMPLE:	(*Bluntly*) Why did you change your mind? Was it because Mark Elliot phoned you?
ROBERT:	Why should he make me change my mind?
TEMPLE:	My wife phoned Elliot this morning – at my request and made an appointment to see him this afternoon. It's my bet Elliot told you about that appointment and you decided to play safe after all and return to the States.
ROBERT:	Play safe? (*Puzzled*) Say, what is this?
TEMPLE:	It was your original intention to see Mrs Russell this afternoon – at five o'clock. You meant to ask her to join your organisation.
ROBERT:	What organisation?
TEMPLE:	(*Slowly*) Dinah Nelson talked, Ferguson – in fact she's still talking …
ROBERT:	Still talking? You're crazy. Dinah's dead!
FORBES:	Oh, no she's not! Elliot thought she was dead – the hospital told him so. But you can take it from me she's very much alive. As much alive as Mackintosh, in fact!
ROBERT:	Do you mean Mackintosh didn't commit suicide?
TEMPLE:	(*Smiling*) I think we'd better let Elliot tell you about Mackintosh. I understood he got quite a shock when he saw him this afternoon.
FORBES:	We've arrested Elliot, and he'll talk, Ferguson, I shouldn't have any illusions on that score.
ROBERT:	(*Suddenly; angry*) Well, he can talk till he's blue in the face, but he was in this business just as much as me or anyone else! It was Elliot that

223

handled the distribution side, he gave Richard his instructions, he told Red Harris what to do, he made Clegley murder Mrs Gulliver so that …

TEMPLE: We know all about that, Ferguson. But you were the brains behind the set-up; you started it, you made all the contacts. You – were – Jonathan!

A pause.

ROBERT: (*Quietly*) How long have you known, Temple – about me, I mean?

TEMPLE: Some little time – but, I just wasn't certain. Then as Rudolf Charles died he said something which confirmed my suspicions.

ROBERT: I see. (*Suddenly*) Temple, there are two things I want you to know. One – my wife wasn't mixed up in this business, towards the end she got suspicious and started to make inquiries, but – believe me – she wasn't mixed up in it.

TEMPLE: Go on …

ROBERT: Secondly, I'm a gambler. I've been a gambler all my life, Temple. I know when I'm beaten. (*He hesitates: in pain*)

FORBES: What is it, Ferguson?

ROBERT: (*Unable to speak*) I … I …

TEMPLE: Is it your heart again?

ROBERT: (*In pain*) Yes, it … goes … like … this … sometimes.

TEMPLE: You'd better sit down.

ROBERT sits down.

ROBERT: I'll be all right, it'll pass … It's just the suspense of waiting and wondering if … (*He is in obvious pain*) Temple, my wife has got some tablets of mine … they're in her handbag. Do

224

you think ... you could ... get one ... for me? They usually do the trick?

TEMPLE: Yes, all right, Ferguson.

The door opens and closes.

FORBES: There's a settee over here, Ferguson. I think you'd better lie down.

ROBERT: No, I'm better sitting up, I – I ... (*In pain*) Gee, this is one ... of the ... worst attacks ... I've had for some time ... (*A moment trying to get his breath*) Do you think I could have ... a drink of water?

FORBES: Yes, there's some water on the desk. I'll get it for you.

ROBERT: Thanks.

A pause.

FORBES pours out a glass of water.

FORBES: Here we are ...

ROBERTS: Thanks.

ROBERT takes the glass and sips the water.

A pause.

FORBES: Is that better?

ROBERT: I think it's easing off a little, but ... (*In pain*) Oh! Gee!!!!

The door opens.

FORBES: Did you get the tablet, Temple?

TEMPLE: Yes. Here it is, Ferguson.

ROBERT: Oh, thanks! Thanks a lot ...

ROBERT swallows the tablet and takes a long drink of water.

A long pause.

FORBES: Feeling better?

ROBERT: I will in a few minutes. (*Slowly; obviously no longer in pain*) Did my wife say anything, Temple?

TEMPLE: No; she just gave me the tablet.

ROBERT: Is – is she o.k.?

TEMPLE: Yes, she's all right.

FORBES: Is the tablet having any effect?

ROBERT: It will, Sir Graham. (*Significantly*) Don't worry
            – it will …

FORBES: (*Suddenly; suspicious*) What do you mean,
            Ferguson?

ROBERT: I told you I was a gambler, didn't I? I told you I
            knew … when … to … throw … in … my …
            chips.

TEMPLE: Yes, well, I'm not a gambler. I never have
            been. Here's the tablet your wife gave me. You
            took an aspirin.

Dramatic FADE UP of music.

Very slow FADE DOWN of music.

*TEMPLE, STEVE and SIR GRAHAM FORBES are sitting in
front of the fire in PAUL TEMPLE's flat.*

TEMPLE: (*Yawning*) By Timothy, I feel tired tonight.

STEVE: Yes – well, you'd better not feel too tired!
            You've both got some explaining to do …

FORBES: What do you mean, explaining, Steve?

STEVE: Well, in the first place, I just don't understand
            why Mackintosh pretended he was Jonathan.

TEMPLE: That was my brainwave, Steve – and since it
            worked I take the credit for it.

FORBES laughs.

TEMPLE: Actually, the idea was to lull Ferguson into a
            feeling of complete security. I put the idea to
            Mackintosh and he agreed to help us. We did
            very much the same sort of thing over Dinah
            Nelson.

STEVE: What do you mean?

FORBES: When Elliot telephoned the hospital he was told that Dinah had died: later the same morning Temple assured him that no one had actually spoken to Dinah.

STEVE: So, he felt on pretty safe ground.

TEMPLE: Very safe ground: so much so in fact that he decided to stay on and form the nucleus of a new organisation with Ferguson. I told Mrs Russell to phone Ferguson and suggest a meeting at the hotel, to give him a pretty broad hint that she was hard up and might be prepared to join the new set-up. Ferguson was rather worried about her – he knew she'd been very friendly with Richard and he wasn't sure just how much she knew. Well, Sir Graham and I kept the appointment instead of Mrs Russell. But of course the Fergusons had already left for the airport.

STEVE: Yes, but I still don't quite see how this business first started.

TEMPLE: Well, as you know, Steve, Ferguson was running a stolen car racket and he employed a number of people including Red Harris, Rudolf Charles, Mrs Gulliver, Richard Ferguson, etc. His right hand man was Mark Elliot. Now several months ago a man called Dumas contacted Ferguson. Dumas was running a car racket on the Continent.

FORBES: And he thought he'd like to tie up with the Jonathan organisation. He probably wanted sterling or dollars. So, he wrote Ferguson a friendly note and sent him a present: the present was the signet ring.

STEVE: I see.

227

TEMPLE: Dumas told Ferguson he was taking no chances and that when they did meet, Ferguson, or his appointed deputy, must wear the ring as a means of identification. But things suddenly began to get very hot for Dumas and the meeting was postponed. Ferguson then gave the ring to Richard without telling him how important it was. But Richard gave the ring to Mavis Russell.

STEVE: That was rather silly of him.

FORBES: When Ferguson arrived in England and discovered that his son had apparently been murdered, and that the ring was missing, he felt sure that Elliot was double-crossing him.

STEVE: He thought that Elliot had murdered Richard and stolen the ring?

FORBES: Yes. But of course Richard had merely made up his mind to get out of the car racket. He phoned his father and explained what had happened. Ferguson was furious and told him he must get the ring back and explained why.

TEMPLE: He was also worried in case someone had overheard that phone call from a man supposed to be dead. So, to cover himself he told me Richard had phoned him, and then made up the story about Richard wanting to meet him at the house in Lewisham.

FORBES: Knowing, of course, that he wasn't at the house and that Red Harris had been taken care of.

STEVE: Yes, that's the night Ferguson had the heart attack and we went in his place.

TEMPLE: Yes.

STEVE: But, Paul, was Richard Ferguson blackmailing Elliot?

TEMPLE: Of course he wasn't. Elliot invented the blackmailing story to explain his association with young Ferguson.

FORBES: Actually, Elliot convinced Jonathan that he had nothing to do with the missing ring and promised that if Ferguson and his wife supported his blackmailing story he'd do his best to get the ring back. In fact he did get it back – he stole it from your husband the night you went to The Encounter.

STEVE: Yes, but why did he give it back to us the next morning?

FORBES: Because Dumas had been arrested the night before …

STEVE: I see … I think. This is complicated. But I think I've got it.

FORBES: Not knowing that Dumas was arrested, Richard still thought the ring was important and got in touch with Temple. Elliot followed young Ferguson out to his car and stopped him. There was an argument and Ferguson was shot. After the murder Elliot parked the car by the side of the road, dashed to the A.A. box and phoned Clegley.

TEMPLE: Clegley was the man who murdered Mrs Gulliver.

FORBES: He told Clegley what had happened and asked him to take care of the body. He certainly did – he set the car on fire.

TEMPLE: Elliot was taking no chances. He'd made up his mind to eliminate anybody who was likely to talk. That included Mrs Gulliver, Mavis Russell and Dinah Nelson. It was Charles who was given the job of disposing of Dinah but unfortunately she turned the tables on him.

STEVE: But, Paul, if she killed Rudolf Charles, Mackintosh must have seen the body!

TEMPLE: He did. When he returned with the aspirin he found Dinah standing over Charles with the revolver in her hand: he disposed of the revolver and told Dinah to get out of Oxford as quickly as she could. She didn't, of course, she tried to commit suicide.

STEVE: But what about the post card she received from Jonathan?

FORBES: It was phoney, Steve. Jonathan knew that we had one genuine card – the card sent to young Ferguson – the others were meant to put us off the scent.

STEVE: Did Mackintosh know that Rudolf Charles was a member of the Jonathan set-up?

TEMPLE: No, he didn't. When we explained the position to him he told us the truth about the Charles murder and agreed to co-operate with us.

STEVE: (*Thoughtfully*) Paul, there's just one other point. Before Rudolf Charles died he said "Ferguson is the ring." What did he mean by that?

TEMPLE: What he <u>tried </u>to say was – Ferguson – meaning <u>Robert</u> Ferguson – Ferguson-is-the-ring-<u>leader</u> …

STEVE: The ring-leader! I never thought of that!

FORBES: No, and your dear husband only thought of it twenty-four hours after Rudolf Charles said it!

They all laugh.

TEMPLE: (*Laughing*) Yes, but I did think of it, Sir Graham!

The laughter gradually dies down.
A slight pause.

FORBES: (*With almost a sigh of disappointment*) Well, that's the end of the Jonathan mystery, Temple.

TEMPLE: (*Jumping up*) Yes, thank goodness, and I want to celebrate it! (*Very gay*) Steve, where's the bottle of champagne? Oh, here we are!

STEVE: Paul, you're not going to open a bottle of champagne at this time of night.

TEMPLE: I certainly am! That's precisely what I'm going to do! This is an occasion, darling! A festive occasion!

TEMPLE opens the bottle of champagne.

TEMPLE: Sir Graham, your glass!

TEMPLE pours the champagne.

FORBES: Thank you, Temple!

STEVE: Steve! Come on, darling! Come on!

TEMPLE pours STEVE a glass.

TEMPLE: Now – I'm going to make a toast!

FORBES: You're going to do nothing of the sort! I'm the oldest member of this trio and if anyone's going to make a toast – I'm going to make it.

A pause.

FORBES raises his glass.

FORBES: To – Paul Temple … and Steve!

TEMPLE: (*Surprised*) What's the matter, darling?

STEVE: I think I'm going to cry …

TEMPLE: By Timothy, women are extraordinary!

They all laugh.

FADE IN of signature tune.

THE END

Introducing Paul Vlaanderen and Ina:
The popularity of Paul Temple in Holland
By **Dick Verwaart**

Anyone in Holland who thinks of the radio serial immediately thinks of Paul Vlaanderen. No other radio serial hero is so engraved in the memory than Vlaanderen. In the fifties and sixties, the AVRO (Algemene Vereniging Radio Omroep) broadcast the radio serials of Paul and Ina (Paul and Steve) on Sunday evenings. The streets were empty and everyone was glued to their radios. After the music of Koos van der Griend, the sonorous voice of the announcer said: "*Paul Vlaanderen and the .... mystery*, a new detective radio serial in eight episodes by Francis Durbridge".

From the speaker we heard the sounds of footsteps on gravel, a squeaking door, howling wind and often a soft moan when Temple found a victim who with the effort of his last breath just couldn't say the name of his murderer.

How well known is the fearful voice of Ina, his wife, who shouted: "Paul!!!!" Reassurance came with the answer: "Ina, darling." They managed to build up the tension to the culmination of the end of each episode. We had to wait another week to see if they managed to get out of their awkward position.

Those who were home alone felt shivers down their spine by the creaking of an open door, or when outside they heard gravel gnashed or a branch slammed against the window.

The British author Francis Durbridge was the creator of Paul and Steve Temple.

Durbridge wrote the first Temple story in 1938.

Send for Paul Temple was broadcast for the first time by the BBC. When the Dutch radio company AVRO bought this series from the BBC, it was thought that Paul Temple was not a Dutch sounding surname at all and they went looking for a

233

Dutch name that fitted better to the imagination of the listeners.

There was a driver with the name Vlaanderen, working for the AVRO. History says that if there were things to be solved inside the AVRO building you only had to ask Vlaanderen and it was done. Thus, the idea was born to call Paul Temple in Holland Paul Vlaanderen and Steve became Ina.

Jan van Ees, who would later play the role of Paul Vlaanderen, first had to settle for a supporting role: Theo Frenkel played the role of Paul and Lily Bouwmeester was Ina.

In February 1939 the series started at the AVRO. It became such a success that the next radio serial was broadcast in April 1939 with the title: *Paul Vlaanderen en de mannen van de Voorpagina* (*Paul Temple and the Front Page Men*). In this, Ina plays an important role.

A year later followed *Paul Vlaanderen en het Z-4 mystery* (*News of Paul Temple*). This was the last radio serial for a while, because during the outbreak of the war, no more radio serials were broadcast.

After the war, the AVRO continued with the radio serials of Temple. In February 1946, *Haal P.V. er weer bij* (*Send for Paul Temple Again*) was broadcast. This time with Jan van Ees as Paul and Eva Janssen as Ina. It became the heyday of the radio serial. In total, 23 Vlaanderen (Paul Temple) radio plays were broadcast.

When Ina at the end of *Send for Paul Temple Again* was knitting a baby sweater Eva Janssen, the Dutch Steve was spontaneously offered a nurse when the time was near.

Baby clothes were sent from all over the country.

Jan van Ees had a hard time on the train, when someone asked how the radio serial would end. The man became angry when Jan van Ees said he didn't know. (And that was true).

234

After the first Temple scripts, that were translated by J.C. van der Horst, Jan van Ees took over the translation under his pseudonym Johan Bennik (Johan Ben Ik) a word joke (Johan Am I).

The last Paul Temple story *Paul Vlaanderen en het Alexmysterie* (*Paul Temple and the Alex Affair*) was broadcast in 1968. With Johan Schmitz as Vlaanderen, because Jan van Ees died in October 1966. Ina (Steve) was then played by Wieke Mulier.

Durbridge had said in an earlier rare interview that he was bored of the Paul Temple character. That was also clear in his last Vlaanderen (Temple) serial.

Certainly not in terms of the structure of the plot, but it was almost an exact copy of a previous serial *Get Paul Vlaanderen back* (*Send for Paul Temple Again*). The name of the criminal Rex was turned into Alex and at the end Ina didn't knit any baby sweaters but she sent Sir Graham Forbes away, in a manner so that Vlaanderen (Temple) didn't have a new case to solve.

In 1967 the EBU (the European Broadcasting Union) commissioned Durbridge to write a thriller in five episodes. The title became *La Boutique* and would be broadcast by all members of the EBU in their own way.

In the meantime, Durbridge had divided his time between writing radio play scripts and television productions. A new period began successfully for him.

If Agatha Christie is called 'Queen of Crime', then Francis Durbridge certainly is 'King of Crime'.

Printed in Great Britain
by Amazon

32130065R00148